THE BIRD HAS

On Saturday, 2 October 2021, 21 writers
in a room and participated in an experiment.
They set out to see if they could write a novel in
24 hours. Birds flew. Rain fell. Last minute
additions brought them up to 22 authors. In the
end, those writers wrote their way up to 60,383
words.
But is it a novel? Well, that's up to you.

What you hold in your hands in the results of that
experiment in its raw form. Every sleepless
missed letter, every mixed up name that existed
at the end of the experiment is here. Does it
function as a novel?

Have a read and find out.

The Bird has Flown

A novel?

Various authors

To Graeme
Best wishes + thanks!
Chap 16 - :)
Debs
x

Hi GRAEME,
THIS IS A BOOK, PROBABLY.
I'M JOE.
J Bunn

THE REAL PRESS

www.therealpress.co.uk

Published in 2022 by the Real Press. www.therealpress.co.uk © The authors.

ISBN (print) 9781912119448
ISBN (ebooks) 9781912119431

Contents

1

Daniel Parsonage

In Search of True Pleasure,
How Vainly We Roam,
To Hold It For Life,
We Must Find It At Home.
The Bird Has Flown.

The message was written three-metres high on his living room wall.

It hadn't been there the night before and the red paint was streaking down from the last stroke of the last 'n'.

It didn't strike him as particularly odd. The wall had been seeping painted messages since the seasons had turned sourly to autumn.

It was certainly an Ominous Message though.

This was one did have something though. A bird. There is always something significant about a bird. Just like a magpie on a rooftop suggests doom and death, a seagull hovering overhead has a clear threat, and an emu in the bathroom suggests hijinks and shenanigans.

There was a time when he had kept birds. We keep birds. Not cats, dog, or lizards. But birds are kept. They need to be kept because they want to fly. And a bird in a cage is no bird at all. Though I suppose that if the bird has flown then maybe it is a better place. The message is a message of hope. The bird that was caged has flown. It is part of a flock or a skein. It is now diving and swooping in the morning sky. Free from whatever cage it had been caught in.

Stafen had always had a connection with birds. Since he'd been a child when the wooden frame had collapsed from his bedroom leaving the complete pane of glass to fall and shatter on the crazy paving below. Silverfish had swarmed from the sodden wood remains on his windowsill. Then small grey birds had gathered to feast. They had picked the sill clean over an hour. Their shrill delight was wonderful. His whole room open to the elements and birdsong. The snapping of beaks and the crunch of the rich thorax meat.

Birds didn't haunt but Stafen couldn't remember a day when he hadn't seen look at him like they knew more than they were letting on. The previous night there had been a robin in the garden casually throwing an empty shell against the kitchen window. It had an arrogant swagger and held its head at an angle. The previous week there had been a thrush loudly chasing a discarded lid across the decking. And one day, a few years back, a golden eagle had taken in a delivery for him and had posted a postcard through his door. Stafen had struck up a friendship with the eagle and for a while they had played squash at the local leisure centre every Wednesday until the eagle had started working nights at the box factory. After that he only saw the eagle on weekends to chat over the garden fence or if Stafen needed some cardboard boxes.

He had lived alone for a while but it had only been for the last few months that messages had started appearing on his wall.   Stafen liked it. At least someone was talking to him.

This message had a certain clarity and a delicious ambiguity.

In Search of True Pleasure
What was true pleasure?

Well there is a certain pleasure in lying in the park covered in trail mix coaxing squirrels to use you as a buffet table. You can taste joy in finding an extra trifle in the fridge then eating it deep at the back of the deepest wardrobe with the longest spoon in the house.

A wise crow once said that the only moment of true pleasure is waking and realising that you don't need to get out of the nest early that day. Just rolling over under the newspaper twigs and getting an extra snooze. But what do crows know?

Stafen had a list that he kept besides his bed. He had written it on a long bus journey from a llama sanctuary to a nearby field where someone had told him that they had lavender that sounded like ragtime when the wind blew from the east. The paper had been torn from a book that had a picture of a hound on the front. One of those sad hounds but this one was wearing a tall wide hat and a yellow cardigan that said 'Cobblers' in bright purple letters. Stafen had taken the blank pages and left the cover on the bus.

When he got home he had torn the sheets into rectangles then on each one he had written something that he liked then glued each strip onto a large A2

5

black card. The strips were poorly glued and at angles but most mornings Stafen would roll over, place his stuffed walrus to one side, then sit bolt upright and read his collage out loud to the windows:

- The one time when you found a feather in a forest and after you picked it up saw that there was a stained-glass window hung between two trees. The light from the rising sun moved slightly and shone through the glass. Then you could see that it was a picture of a turkey.
- The moment when young child next door gave up learning to play the bassoon.
- A ball bearing settling perfecting in a ball bearing sized hole
- A panda diligently eating a forest of bamboo then dozing off and rolling onto its back in ecstasy.
- The taste of pick and mix when you just bought it for yourself on a rainy afternoon when you were supposed to be working
- That time when you needed to do some laundry and thought you would have to go out and get some laundry liquid but just as you put your coat on remembering that you bought two bottles last time so the second one is at the back of the cupboard
- A well stacked dishwasher
- The tick of an old clock in a large hall
- Trying a new book by a new author from the local library and finding that it is a book about sentient spiders that speak to you from the page
- A large plant that you notice one morning has sprouting a new leaf

6

- A cat that chose to sit on your lap

But are any of this true pleasure?

Was the message telling to seek something more?

Or was it more about vainly roaming? Roaming with vanity or in vain?

Stafen had certainly roamed. He had been to places. Some nearby places like the pigeon memorial in town – dedicated to the warrior birds who had carried messages during the wars. Small birds darting from the trenches across the seas and home. He liked to sit on a bench by the memorial and watch the pigeons gather on the stones. This was because it was not just a statue to pigeons – it was garden for pigeons and about pigeons. A little pigeon sanctuary with a little pigeon garden. The pigeons had their own space to remember their dead. That was why he watched. He roamed to the pigeon memorial and watch the pigeon roam in their safe space. He felt safe watching them.

Sometimes he roamed further. He liked airports. He like the process. The vainglorious illusion of safety. Flying to a town much like his own but with different signs and different food. A local interest museum with local interests. Different local interests from a different locality.

He had once travelled to a Swedish town and to a cardboard factory looking for a particular cardboard box for the neighbourhood eagle.

It was an adventure and it involved roaming...

Stafen had stood on the forecourt of the Q8 garage that stood between the apartment block he lived in and the mysterious and slightly annoying warehouse with its illuminated sign. The warehouse had two obvious entrance points – a main corrugated steel door and a wooden side door. Stafen had been at the garage for over an hour and had had to pop into the shop to purchase liquorice and car-shaped sweets. He had formulated and unformulated his plan three times, essentially, he was going to stride in looking authoritarian and demand an explanation.

The trouble was he lacked authority. He had never even been able to command a hypothetical in-bred of dog to sit. It wasn't his lack of height, scruffiness, or even his voice; but rather it was just him. Everything about him lacked authority. He could wait at a bar remaining un-served and thirsty until everyone else had been sated. In Sweden with its fondness for table service, this had been slightly ameliorated, but his table was frequently ignored nevertheless. He never complained as he knew that no-one would listen. This is the opposite of true: he always complained. About everything, under his breath, you could hear him muttering about:

- The general unfairness of life
- The inferior scripts in modern cinema
- The fact that it was still considered odd to ask for a mixture of sweet and salty popcorn
- The way everyone went on holiday at the same time
- The fondness of Swedes for putting béarnaise sauce on pizza
- His lack of a driver's licence
- The way that women scorned him before he had

even had a chance to merit it

- Modern swimming pools refusing to be rectangular
- Trying to create any kind of chart or table in MS Word without smashing your monitor with a hammer
- The fact that the universe had overlooked his evident genius and he was stuck in Q8 forecourts staring at warehouses.

The last point annoyed him. He had annoyed himself by his indecision. He decided to take positive action, and after popping back into the garage shop to get a boiled hot dog, a can of low strength beer, a can of medium-strength beer, and a packet of Prince cigarettes, he strode around the roundabout and discovered that there was no pedestrian access from the dual carriageway that interjected between his house and the warehouse, and the industrial estate where the warehouse in question seemed like the only still occupied building. Shimmying down the grass bank through the brambles; carrying a can of lager in one hand, and a carrier back containing a can of lager in the other, his cigarette in his mouth had gone out due to the rain that had started as soon as he had stepped out of his cover, and his clothes were getting torn and dirty; he considered the fact that he had truly not wanted anything more in his life than to see what was inside the warehouse.

Emerging from the bushes looking even more bedraggled than he usually did, he stood up to his full height and dusted himself down in that way people do as expected by the audience. He walked with a new

9

assurance towards the wooden side door (he was more confident than usual but still didn't fancy brazening his way through the main entrance). He was up to the wooden door. Now he was close to the warehouse its sheer scale impressed him. He wasn't terribly experienced in the ways of warehouses, but this seemed to his untrained eye, fucking massive. Like IKEA but grey and sad: lacking the bright false joy of the friendly corporation.

The door had no handle (evidently it was supposed only to be opened from the inside), but it was slightly ajar. The wood had splintered due to the weather, and it was easy to gain a handhold. Stafen carried out all of these actions on autopilot. He had decided to enter the warehouse and even the signs on the car park that said 'utfart', and 'infart' had only stopped him for a brief slightly xenophobic snigger (in fact through his time in Sweden he had only failed to laugh at these signs on this occasion and one when he was in an ambulance arriving at A&E with a man who had fallen in a threshing machine).

He pushed the door with confidence only to find that it would only open ten centimetres at most. There was evidently something wedged behind, cramming his head through the gap he was met with a wall of cardboard. The boxes were about a metre cubed and were not that heavy but the rain that had leaked through the door had soaked the bases and meant they would no longer slide across the floor. Using his minimal might he shoved his way through causing the boxes to buckle but gaining entry. He was now standing encased in cardboard surround by the thought: "what now?" Technically his plan had only gone as far as entering the warehouse.

After approximately fifteen minutes in the dark (he had passed the time by humming the them to Ski Sunday to himself) he decided he could not just leave, and he could not go forwards he must go up. Gripping the corner of the next box up, he started to climb. As the boxes crumpled, they made rudimentary stairs. As he got higher, the air got colder and colder with ice crystal forming on the boxes. Moss and bracken were attached to them, making his grip harder to maintain. The air was thin, and breathing became so tricky he forced to extinguish his third cigarette and concentrate on not dying due to altitude sickness. After time had lost all meaning and the boxes became encased in snow and ice he reached a plateau. Up here there was no sense of the ceiling that must be present, but a few paces away from where he emerged was what can only be considered to be AN OMINOUS PORTAL

A bird flew out from the portal.

He had roamed away from the ominous portal.

He had roamed to the Arctic and seen an elk.

He had roamed in the desert and sheltered in the shade of a lone tree.

He had stood in the rain near a busy motorway.

He had stayed in a hotel where the staff were all chickens.

He had caught a meteorite straight out of the sky whilst paying for a hot dog outside a department store.

Had he been vain in these moments? Or had these

moments been in vain? Moments in life with pure pleasure and times where he had roamed possibly in vain.

Perhaps, it was in vain because it was at home he needed to be content.

To hold it for life we must find it at home

And home was this house.

And home was his body. The meat machine he operated.

These days his body made ominous signs. It was a

His house creaked at night and the windows rattled.

He was thirty years old but he looked older. Years of starting at blank walls hoping for messages; ominous or otherwise.

Maybe home was the pure pleasure. His cupboard had food in it. His taps produced water. He was over supplied with books. And on his walls, he had pictures of the places he had roamed.

But maybe it was a warning. Maybe his bird had flown. The pure pleasure had left and he had to be content in his home.

He was gaunt and lost like a vacant boarded up tower block. His dull and dead. His hand shock when he drank his morning coffee. He was a wreck. If this was his home then he found no pleasure in it.

He stalked through his home to the kitchen. There was no bird at the window and the sky was silent.

Stafen pulled open the fridge door and heard the rattled of the glass bottles before he looked inside.

Thousands of birds rushed out. Starlings first beating their wing against the stale interior air. They filled the kitchen nagging against the recessed lighting looking for a portal to the sky. Stafen fending in lethargic panic as their wings beat his face. Accidentally pecks left blood spots. Then the gulls came. From deep within the fridge huge gulls with curved sweet beaks knocking Stafen back against the opposite wall. Their hard faces angry and distressed. They squawked and called to each other shared the rage amongst the flock. The starlings find themselves crowded out by the gulls all rushed to the corner by the microwave knocking over unused recipe books and cereal boxes. The starlings formed a spiralling cloud in one corner whilst the gulls shot in chaos around the room. Some headed down the corridor and he could hear the pecking of plaster and masonry from elsewhere in the house. Then, as the blood coursed down his face, Stafen blink away to see wide winged hawks burst out of the salad drawer. These birds just beat him aside and onto the floor by the dining table. They formed a flying carpet covering the ceiling and darkening the room. In panic now, the starling surged to the closed kitchen door. Some of the gulls had found the bread bin and had pushed it off the surface so that it split open and a cloud of mould had spewed out leaving the rotten bread opened and then consumed within seconds. Other gulls were trying to see if they could get residue from the dishes pilled here and there by the sink.

They cracked the plates and bowls with shards of porcelain flying across the room piercing gulls and starling, shooting them from the sky. The drum beat of dying birds falling against the tiles created a thunder

13

that rivalled the pounding wings. Stafen, now slumped against the cold radiator, raised his head once more. Opening his eyes, a crack he saw the pink stained sight of the tall feathered necks of the emus untangling themselves from the freezer drawer. Cracking upright they shock the frost from their legs and formed a phalanx with lowered beaks like arrows. As one they charged with elegant silence past Stafen and torn the PVC back door from its frame. Silverfish swarmed unnaturally from the spilt panels.

The emus left the building. Leaving cold wet prints across the tiles. The kestrels folded their wings and dived from the ceiling and gathered the fallen warrior birds from the floor and in one parabolic movement followed the emus out into the garden. A series of regular crashes told of falling garden fences along the terraces as the emus found freedom. The kestrels following like an avian blitzkrieg. Then the gulls sensed the bugle call to advance and left, but not ordered like the previous waves but in dribs and drabs, seagull by seagull. Some still holding globules of wet bread remains. From the other room the gulls returned; stained red and dusted with white. Finally, the starling cyclone spiralled through the room and out of the portal. They circled the garden sending leaves and moss scattering. Then they too left.

Stafen scraped blood and dirt from his face. Pushed himself up against the wall and dabbed his wounds with the tea towel that was illustrated with a cat dressed as an astronaut.

He looked at the open fridge with the salad drawer thrown clear and the freezer drawer jammed open.

Inside, there was a pigeon. It looked at him as if equally bewildered by recent events. The pigeon hopped down from the condiment shelf and down onto the floor, then trotted out of the kitchen. Stafen followed it down the dark corridor to the living room lit only by the stripes between the closed venetian blinds. The pigeon awkwardly got onto the sofa and nestled down between the cushioned. Stafen dropped down beside it and they both looked at the wall opposite.

The gulls had hacked the wall and chunks of plaster and stone covered the floral carpet. The message was gone besides the last four words.

"The bird has flown"

He stroked the pigeons soft feathered and it coos calmed him.

The pigeon shared a moment of pure pleasure in their home.

2

Liz Eastwood

Metaphysical Soldier
Jenny

It was the second Saturday in a row. Someone had
taken a lot of care. Neatly cutting words from the
Observer and My Waitrose Food Magazine. The first
time, it was '*In search of true pleasure?*' It was quite
amusing, but no sex toy special offers. We jumped into
bed. Not a total success, but kind of pleasurable.
Seven out of ten. I didn't often give Rick a seven. He
tried hard, but it was a bit of a slog at times. Maybe my
scars and prosthetics put him off. Tony was better, but
he was military. He got it. But then he just upped and
left. The wife called the Salvation Army Missing
Persons hot line. Poor Yvonne, she couldn't accept
he'd gone off her. The second time it was '*How vainly
we roam.*'

I dug the first one out of the recycling. It could
have been a joke. The last one was, '*The bird has
flown.*' In order of receipt, over the next three
Saturdays, the messages read:

In search of true pleasure,
How vainly we roam,

To hold it for life,
We must find it at home.
The bird has flown

The last thing, on Saturday March sixteenth two thousand and nineteen was a bouquet on the doorstep. Dried desert flowers, hawthorn, honeysuckle and foul-smelling asafoetida. The card was inscribed *Bird has Flown* in thick deep purple calligraphy. The Deep Purple CD was wrapped in a yellowed nineteen forty-two army field newspaper. Another crazy war, more young men wasted away.

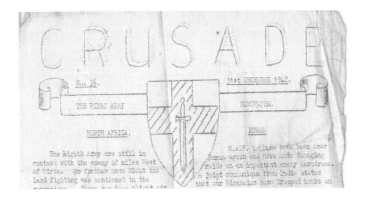

Those cuttings were from my regular newspapers. Who knows about me? Only Dan, but he's dead. Blown away by friendly fire in Afghanistan. My falcon, my Lannah, she knew but she died. My head blows. I want to die. My Glock Seventeen pistol is in the attic, safely hidden. Why did I survive, when Dan and Two Sheds and our squaddies were blown away? Their bits will never come home. I put the CD on my Groove player, stick it in my pocket. I climb the stairs, pull the loft ladder down.

'And the bird has flown, to a place on its own, somewhere all alone

Lannah: Its three thirty on afternoon of March sixteenth two thousand and nine.   They call me Lannah. It's my fourteenth birthday. I peer through heavy Steiner US Military binoculars. They're mine; I found them after battle over US Army/Afghan base at Wanah.

Atasha, my brother, was civilian trainee. He still got killed. He can't give me food now. I'm disguised as boy. I'm scared. So far, I've counted thirteen nights, sleeping in caves, on these rugged mountains. Through gnarled trees I spy your sand and white combat camouflage. Later, you tell me you're twenty-eight years old and you are army medic, Lance Corporal Jennifer Foxwell.   How calm you seem, as you apply tourniquet to Corporal Dan Thompson's wounds.   Red hot shrapnel has torn gaping holes in his arms, legs and buttocks.   His pulsing flesh is out - like bloody entrails of freshly gutted chicken.

'That will stop the blood flow. I'd give you another painkiller but ... err, do you remember anything?'

'On patrol, anti-tank mine, Two Sheds – sorry Lance Corporal Peters – tried sorting it ... noise deaf ... grenades over the wall ... I ... sorry I can't ... Taliban ...Tony ...'

It's your third month in Afghanistan. You are thinking what to write – and not write - to your mum. Doris cried with pride at the passing out parade, when her Jenny was awarded the dark blue beret of the Royal Army Medical Corps. Will her girl be true to the cap badge motto – *IN ARDUIT FIDELIS* - faithful in adversity? Can your far away mum imagine my rugged, arid desert dotted with camel thorns, locoweed, spiny rest-harrow, euphoric scented mimosa?

Later, you plan to email your brother; attach pictures of bitterns, herons and grebes. Birds are fewer and fewer here in my Kunar River Valley; don't tell brother. He'd only say *it's the chemicals, it's the filthy war*. Your friend, Jamie Peters was teaching you plant medicine. It would have been wild wormwood next. Pity he was such a bloody hero, defusing roadside bomb. Your mum doesn't need to know about arms trafficking, drug smuggling or incendiaries. My desert is far from Doncaster, River Don and your home in Don Valley. I'll tell you that bad uncle raped me. I can't go back to my village. They'd make me marry him – or stone me to death.

Before I see US war plane, I smell gas. My shout – 'نگاه کردن ، این بمب' – *look out it's a bomb*, is too late. Grey ash culls creatures. The burning mimosa releases a fractured fragrance of Atasha calling to me in opaque ancient Farsi. The 'duh, duh' of explosion deafens me. Explosive heat sears sand black, floodlighting whole field hospital camp with blinding red, yellow and blue friendly fireworks. Is pilot proud of his artful precision? His Flight Eagle blasts spheres, cubes, black fragments into Red Cross, slicing so exactly on its axis.

We morph into one soundless scream, a black circling smoky gulp of scarlet flaming metallic volcanic eruptions - scaling scenic mountain scarps, cutting scary blood burnt copper, gashing golden contradictions of black cinders, creating chromatic photovoltaic tongues of earth, wind and fire elemental power to gushing, rushing red rivers over-blooding. Our twin souls shudder still.

You lie on hot sand with your chest ripped open, a strange alabaster and amber glow colours the skeletal clavicle. Red desert sun sets and moon rises instantly, like orange balloon at our party.

Your chest is pretty badly burnt up; I smell charred black bones. You're still. Silence is deafening. Feels like we're more than likely dead; our souls go walkabout. We fly skywards, a single surreal solar sound wave. Fiery wind curves, like migrating heron soaring on the diagonal way beyond sun to strangely cooler climes. How can River Don be after Hindu Kush? And surely it can't be Himalayas next.

We need to stop, ask for directions. We are one grain of sand caught in a high speed curved magnetic field. We crash land. Now I am Lannah, graceful black and grey feathered falcon. You see my creamy white throat, reddish brown crown with your one eye. I break monitor lizard's neck. Eat what I can, but not head

'Why did you kill my brother?' I ask.

'But, I didn't. I couldn't even kill an animal. How bad am I? Dan? Tony? Tony?'

Your words scramble, but I understand.

'Half your face is meat and your right leg is gone and ...'

'... ok, it's a bit of a bloody mess. Are we dead?'

Inside my head pictures come and go; I dream of black-bearded men and white horses galloping and Strike Hawk hunting me. Don't catch me, don't chain me, don't cover my head then drug me and cage me. I can't be sold; a slave, I can't submit to my uncle. Let me fly to red crescent moon, free from purdah.

'Let me die. Don't want to be an ugly disfigured cripple; *no ... mean disabled.*'

I'm dreaming blind, begging for answers. I hear that you joined army to get money, get career, look after child; it's better than NHS. Blood stripes the cherry red, royal blue and gold of your medical services belt. Your Two Rifles Battalion cap badge is dented. I fly to River Kunar, pick soothing sour purple fruits from black plum tree. I cover you in its small fragrant flowers. Then our souls can fly. We are one. We are Lannah. My wide wings speed on, at hundred miles an hour; we don't need map.

I stoop, we power dive into your dream. It's four o' clock on morning of seventeenth March two thousand and one. We're looking down on maternity unit of Doncaster Royal Infirmary. You tell mum *fuck off,* one last push, then Sophie squishes out. *Sorry mum.*

'Mum, how will I cope? I'm no good with babies. Can't I come and live with you and Rick?'

'There's no room for screaming kids in that poky little flat. Besides, the fourteenth floor is a long way if the lift ...'

You move in with big sister Chris and her partner, Tina. The next year you've started an access to nursing course. Tina shares childcare.

'... but look Chris, even as a student I'd get sixteen thousand a year and the army pay for the student accommodation and ...' you didn't want to be any kind of ordinary nurse.

'Alright, but Birmingham is a long way. The information pack says you "do extra training in the holidays and some weekends ... once you qualify you go straight to your first posting." ' Tina hugs Sophie to her, like she's the mother.

'I know it's a lot to ask. I want to pay my way, have my own place. Chris, please – the army guarantees me a proper job.' Chris gives in – as usual.

You go to Winchester for field and combat training; four weeks away from home. It's pretty tough. You're star trainee at Queen Alexandra's Royal Army Nursing Corps; you love student life.

'... he's really nice ... teaching Field First Aid ... been for a drink a few times. Can you put Sophie on? My battery's low. My class starts in two mins.'

'Tina's taken her to Ben's birthday party. Watch out with men; don't get too involved. Sophie is one thing, but don't ...'

You tell me *they* don't need you. Auntie Tina is her real mummy. I cling to you, desperately running disjointed dream movies of your life.

Sophie is star. Tina pushes her on trike to Sandall Park. They've got bag of toast and marmite crusts for ducks. They jump in puddles, chase fluffy cygnets. Sophie squeals as swans nip at her. At home they curl up on sofa, eating crisps and chocolate, laughing at Charlie and Lola on wide screen telly. Auntie Tina reads stories and Sophie climbs into her bed again that night. Chris walks the two miles to her work at Duchess of York art house cinema. She loves teaching students to tell stories with visual effects and animation in film.

On New Year's Eve two thousand and six, Chris invites you to preview a short.

'She's nearly six. I want to take her to the viewing.' Sophie clings to Tina.

'She's too young, she won't understand.' Chris isn't going to shift.

You cry inside, pretend you don't mind. It's just few months after Iraq tour, few days before you leave for Afghanistan.

'I've used multi cameras to make a shape shifting dream sequence; the star turns into a falcon, then flies away. We do miss you little Jenny wren.' Chris puts protective arm round you.

'It reminds me of Kafka. Is it Metamorphosis? This salesman is a beetle when he wakes up – ugh! Sorry I'll be away for your birthday ...' smiles, tears, hugs.

Do Tina and Chris sense a faint echo of wounded soldier and her hawk-eyed nurse as we fly on?

23

'I don't remember the end of Kafka story. Why am I flying around looking at myself? Am I dead yet? Dan, Tony?'

We dream on. You're ten. Chris is twenty-two. It's Christmas day nineteen ninety-three. Dad is still alive. He lost job at car factory this year, but they paid him off. So you find loads of presents under tree. The best ones are Western Stamping Barbie Doll and her Western Star Horse with his brown curling 'real' mane. You tie Barbie's blond hair in high ponytail wish Star was real.

Chris gives you nurse uniform and some army stuff. She shows you how to hold gun and ties strings of white nurse apron and takes your photo with her new camera. I feel fearful when I see how the holy red marker crosses your heart.

'Look, I'm a nurse soldier. Barbie and Star are in Bosnia. Her leg's been blown off by a land mine.'

Dad is annoyed that the doll is broken, but mum tops up his wine, telling him that their little medic will make it good as new.

'We never did find that leg again. It must have been thrown out, with the Christmas wrapping paper. Poor dad, we didn't know it was his last Christmas – bloody lung cancer – and all I could do was moan on about not having a real horse. Oh God, I hate myself. I want to die, it hurts too much. Where are we? Help me. I didn't set out to kill anyone. Forgive me.'

24

I check your body. I count three nights, since I've kept you alive in my desert. I peck and spit at asafoetida, place warm soothing stinky gunk of plant medicine in your open chest. You can't eat with your half mouth, so I peck and spit at shrew and gently feed you globs. You still want to die; I won't let you. I feed you wild poppy seeds and peck insects and puss off wounds. We get high and fly through future stars, through crazy trees, through fiery desert winds.

Its seventeen days after friendly fire incident. We find you in Birmingham Selly Oak Hospital for injured military personnel. I fold wings, perch on windowsill. We peer through fog into white room. You're linked to silver machines, with orange tubes poking out. Chris, Tina, mum, Craig, Lance Corporal Jamie Peters, Corporal Dan Thompson, Western Stamping Barbie, Star, Atasha and Kafka are crying. The army medic points the remote control at red-cross target on your chest. She's going to turn you off.

'But the lover whose bird has flown, catches nothing only grains of sand.

A deep male voice sings along to Deep Purple. He sobs, can't keep going.

Jenny: "Now the hermit in his lonely cave has himself to keep him company.'

I stop the CD. My Glok is ready. Should I leave a note? I can't think. Tony? Who is Sophie? I want to die, but I lie here alone in the dark. Lights above me. I smell burnt. My legs are heavy. Why can I hear Tony? He was blown away. He must have been, the whole camp was destroyed by the Americans. I think so, but what is happening?

'No, no please don't switch her off. She's got to live. Her child.'

'All the children in the distant house, they have feelings only children know.'

Tony sings close to my ear. I must be hallucinating. Maybe that bouquet was toxic. Somebody has killed me after all, so no need for the Glok. With only one leg, one arm, one eye and my crazy flashbacks they have done me a favour. I'll never get Sophie away from Tina and Chris now. They will be better for her. I never should have joined up and left her with them. She needs a proper mum. Tina loves her. It's no good saying we can parent her between us. The poor kid will be so confused. That's the bad thing, if I die now I'll never see her again. She's already lost her dad, so I crawl towards the ladder. Must make an effort to find an antidote. Drop the Glock. I want to live.

'Don't die. You mustn't kill yourself. Sophie needs you.'

I wriggle down the ladder, head bleeding from a gunshot like I am a snake. My tongue flicks out, I can't call out. The ladder has turned in to desert sand. It's too hot, my blood stains the desert. How can I get it clean? Help me, I must be drugged. I lie on my bed, but it isn't in my bedroom. It is hard, it slopes up and the sheets are white. My duvet is gone. The curtains are all wrong. Where's my bedside Kindle? I am under canvas, in the desert camp. Teaching Tony how to apply a tourniquet.

Why send such a novice to a dangerous war zone? He said he'd always wanted to be a nurse and the army gave him a chance in life. Everyone else gave up on him. He was such a good sort. We didn't do anything unprofessional. He said it would be nice to meet when we got back to the UK. Off duty, of course. I told him about Sophie and my wild times. He had been a bit of a lad, but his mum died of cancer when he was sixteen. Strangely, that calmed him down. He didn't want to cause his dad any more grief. So, he joined up as soon as the army would take him. I slid off the ladder altogether and it morphed into a bed.

Lannah: 'Mummy, mummy... I want my mummy ...' Sophie sees us at window. She flies into the intensive care room. Nurses try to hold her back. She shoves them aside, grows to six foot two and overshadows the whole room. It is black dark except for a luminous red cross above the bed. It is totally silent apart from the sound of a US Army drone. She throws you a lucky star bouquet of seven heliotropes, seven carnations, seven opium poppies and seven violets. You want to live. On day four, an army patrol finds you in my desert, covered in fragrant plum flowers and stinking of asafoetida. I soar into fiery Red Crescent moon, scorching to earthly death, raining all the fragments of my soul into your chest.

'The bird has flown. To a place on its own. Somewhere all alone.'

We live. Sometimes - when no one knows - we fly to my desert.

3
Vanessa Cornford

I have taken to night walking. Which is silly because I won't find it in the dark. At least I don't think I will because I'm not entirely sure what I'm looking for. She told me what it said and which town to find it in but she might have been speaking in metaphor or lying, though she didn't usually do either. It always goes the same way; I talk to her in my head, she answers, we argue and laugh and do our routines and it never makes me feel better. Closer to her a little but not better.

I'm fatter than before. Because of what happened to us, then me, and then what happened to all of us. So now walking around the town trying to find it, is also an exercise thing. Walk, look, think, search, walk, think about her, check how many steps, think about what I'm looking for, think about getting fatter, think about was it a message or a joke or a goodbye of sorts.

'Go live there I liked it there. It was a fun day. Go live there and when you are there look for where it says a thing about how to live and where to find a home. I saw it when we were there that day. The bird has flown.'

It felt a little like poetry but it was also the drugs

29

and they were giving her and i was tired and scared and didn't want to think of any time when I would do any thing in any place where she was not. But she was dying and so we didn't know where she would be and I wouldn't know how to find her. My sister.

There were always missions to do and I had to do them cos she was the big sister and I the little one. Once she told me she saw this girl with these amazing shoes and didn't know what they were called and had not seen them before or since and really wanted a pair. Could I find them? And so I did. I found them. I found what they were called I found the colour she wanted I found where we could buy them and we did. The exact same ones she had seen and I hadn't. Lots of little missions over lots of years and this now the last one.

So I live here now, by the sea, in the town we stopped over for a day. If the message is real, if somewhere there is something saying something about home and about a bird, then she could only have seen it around the places we wandered that day we visited, in the town we took the train to and shopped and had some food all those years ago.

I retrace our steps as best as I remember but I am looking further afield now though I'm not sure why. I've looked in the pier which we didn't visit. I've looked all around the train station where we got off unsure how to get to the town. I've looked on the big ferris wheel by the sea which didn't even exist when we were there. I want to go on it and look from above for the thing about how to live and where to find a home. And something about a bird. But I don't like heights and whatever she told me to find in the town she told me to go live in, cannot be that big that you would see it from the sky. I don't think so.

When I'm walking and searching for the message I have to find, I think about our grandmother walking. She never told us this, our mother did. She told us about grandmother walking all the way from Turkey to Greece a long time ago. My grandmother was just a child and didn't want to go but they had to. And in any case there were the ones coming from the other direction and they had to swap places and houses and lives but never meet. Go, they were told, get to the homeland and whatever you have here, you will find there but better. Lots of countries had decided this was best.

And so they did. They took boats I guess, though I don't know about that bit, and walked. Walked and walked. People died on the way. They buried them and kept walking cos no one wanted them there anymore but everyone was waiting for them where they were going. They just had to walk and get there. Except when they did, no one wanted them there either.

I have found other things on my walks here. Blue plaques with names of writers trying to bind time. Trying to tell us it still matters; this place is what matters not the time. Jane Austen stayed here and so this has something to do with you now. Oscar Wilde here, Pinter over there. At one time in this place that you are now walking by, someone did something big and important and somehow it still lives here. I want a blue plaque for my sister. *My sister came here and we did some shopping and we walked around. Then, years later, I think she told me to move here and look for something*, it would say.

There are benches here too, on the seafront. Benches that tell you who was there and maybe who loved this place that cares about the gone so much. And sometimes they tell you who loved them, the names on the bench. I sit on them sometimes on my walks but I don't understand them. Where I am from in a town far from here where my sister sent me, we don't need reminding of the past and the old. It's everywhere, the very, very old is in the town, in the places and the air and in the way we still think about ourselves. There are ancient bits in the city where I am from, they are everywhere and sometimes get in the way of the new. Sometimes they make us feel like we are the past and don't have to try that hard anymore. Sometimes they make us feel big and proud as if the past has anything to do with us. But where I am now is newer than my city and cares about the past differently. Here is starting to feel like home but not all the time.

In my walks I have seen the pigeon place too. I thought for a little while maybe, that is what my sister meant though we never particularly cared about pigeons so it can't be. It is a memorial to pigeons near the sea. War pigeons that died carrying messages that meant something important to someone at some time. It says 'a bird of the air shall carry the voice and that which hath wings shall tell the matter'. When I saw it I thought maybe that is what my sister meant by 'the bird has flown'. Maybe she saw it that day and I didn't and it meant something. Maybe she was telling me that there was a message that she would send through

32

time and that I would read it and know what to do. But then I thought some more and I don't think that's it. The memorial is to the dead birds. Their messages never made it to where they meant to go. It is for the birds that carried the voice but never told of the matter. Surely that's what that means. They tried to tell but couldn't because they died. War pigeons, love pigeons, carrier pigeons. I feel for them, I do, they died carrying others' voices and others' matters that had nothing to do with them and their pigeon lives. I don't think this is what my sister meant.

I don't remember everything we did that day, years ago, when we were here my sister and I. I don't remember if we were here as sisters or mothers or wives. I don't remember if it was just us. We did shopping but I don't remember what we bought. It was just another day and then we took the train back away from the town. I wish I could find a plaque that reminded me of everything we did that day. And the little things we said. Whether I'd made her laugh, or whether I complained about waiting for her in the shops. I wish it could tell me what we ate and where we walked and what we looked at and pointed at to each other. I think we were happy that day for nothing much but I don't really remember.

On my walks to find the thing my sister said is about how to live and find a home and about a bird that's flown I sometimes think about the story of the girl. The girl in Paris who walked and walked and walked and walked to find her mother that was there one minute and not the next. I've read it a few times and heard it another. The girl and her mother are visiting Paris and the mother gets ill where they are staying. So the girl leaves though she doesn't want to leave her ill mother, but must go find some medicine or a doctor. And when she returns to the place her mother was lying ill and maybe dying, her mother is not there. No one recognises her, no one remembers her or her mother and they send her away. At first the girl thinks she got it wrong because she doesn't know Paris. Or maybe they had just got there I'm not sure it is a while ago I last heard the story.

When the girl is sure that this is the right street, the right place, the right room she is still not there. Everyone tells the girl she was never there in that house, in that room on that street that she returns to. They tell her there was never a girl and never a mother and no one visited and no one got ill. And so the girl roams and roams the streets of Paris for ever and ever with the medicine for her mother who is no longer there, was never there and nobody remembers. I'm not sure if that is better than a mother who has died. I often think of that story or as much as I can remember of it. I don't think my sister would have liked it.

The nightwalks have stopped. It is not safe to walk at night. It never was.

In the day though I still look for the message that my sister told me to find. I see secret messages on walls in the town, there is writing and changing graffiti and paintings and some sneaky street names that feel like they should mean something but they don't. After what happened to all of us there are empty shops with abandoned objects you can see in the shop window and feel like they are saying something. The shopkeepers abandoned the shops and maybe left the town but left some clues to the past or the future for us to see. Little museums, for little things, that lasted a little while. But they are not it and I don't really know what they mean. Sometimes here feels like home and sometimes I think I too have walked here from very, very far away and no one was here waiting for me. To be from another place in every place you go, is always hard.

I think there are secrets in this town too that try to stay hidden. I think under the blue plaques there are other ones that tell of older times and darker things. Things that happened at sea and things that happened by the sea but I'm not sure and anyway that's not what I'm looking for.

There are so many places to eat in this town now. There didn't used to be. One next to the other and the other and one more a little further down. Food from here and there and somewhere far away... You'd think the people here are always hungry and cannot walk too far before they need to eat again. You'd think no one can go anywhere anymore and so the food is the only way to get to faraway places. She liked to eat out my sister.

Sometimes I think the message wasn't real and I am roaming and the roaming is the message. It was off hand, it wasn't the last message, there was no last message. Though she did say 'go live there, I liked it there. Find the thing that said something about how to live and have a home and the bird has flown'. And I think, were you the bird my sister? Did you know, you must have known, did you mean you have flown though you didn't for a little while yet? Or was it fuzzy and a little bit confused and half a dream and half a message?

Where I am from, all our old stories have birds in them. Birds that keep secrets and know things they can't really know. The birds tell tales and travel and gossip and whisper things in people's ears that make the stories happen. They don't carry the messages like the pigeons but they speak. Out loud not chirping tweeting or whatever it is that birds do. They speak in human voices and speak of terrible things. You learn these folk tales at school and then forget about them mostly. In one, the bird whispers in the masterbuilder's ear and kills his wife. The masterbuilder is building a bridge that always falls at night. Over and over until the bird tells him that for the bridge to stand the masterbuilder's wife needs to lie in it. Lie in it and hold it up. That is the only way. And so the story goes and so the master builder does. He sends for her and tricks her and gets her down to the foundations and builds the bridge around his surprised still -loving wife. And not once in the story does anyone ask how did the bird know? Who told the bird, who sent the bird and why did it speak like it spoke? But the bridge does stand I think in the story so I guess the bird was right. It's real this bridge in a real place I have been to. I don't remember the place much or the bridge but I do remember the story.

Was that what my sister meant? The bird has flown and bad things are about to happen? Because it wasn't really a surprise. We knew, we both kind of knew what was coming. We'd known for a while I guess though we still had faith in life and the drugs. Horrid little birds with horrid little voices meaning no good. Not here though. Here birds at worst eat your chips on the beach and help win wars and sing in the forest so you can spot them. Here birds are noble and mysterious and they don't cause much trouble in the stories I don't think.

Today it didn't stop raining. Not even for a bit. Heavy angry rain fighting with the wind for attention. Kind of rain you have to give into and give up to. It's strange here when it rains so much by the sea. Like some secret fight going on that we are in the middle of with our little raincoats and umbrellas; like it's about us when it isn't. And I walked in that rain with someone new from a place where we were telling stories. We walked nearby to a little street that leads to the sea. I think all streets here lead to the sea. It's that kind of place. We walked only for a little bit in that wind and rain towards a message in a stone on the ground she wanted to show me from her story. The stone was old, though we didn't know how old and it had a message carved in it. Just there, on the pavement of this little street across a pub by a house. Further down there were shops with old things and more places to eat. The stone in the pavement had grass growing around it and moss and some of it was chipped away. The message was half there and half we put together. It said something about true pleasure and life and home. And I thought I found it. The thing my sister told me to look for at the place she told me to move to. I couldn't read it all but between us we made it out somehow. *In search of true pleasure, how vainly we roam, to hold it for life, we must find it at home*. It didn't say about a bird.

Today, all day it hasn't stopped raining. And so after we found the message in the stone in the pavement in the street by the pub, I have stayed at home. And I have thought and thought and decided that this is the message. I took a photo of the stone and will say that this is what my sister meant and I can now start walking to places instead of around them.

That was earlier today. Earlier today, I thought I found it. Now I'm not so sure. She wouldn't have seen that little message in the pavement and remembered and thought to tell me so long after. And in any case the message is not in the language we spoke to each other. I don't think she sent me here for this. For this message, about pleasure and finding it at home. It made sense earlier but not anymore. I'm not sure about pleasure and I'm not sure about home. And whatever it means I don't think that is what my sister meant. And in any case it does not mention a bird. Not once.

4
Elaine Ruth White

Darling, I know how you love a mystery – the Eastbourne incident comes immediately to mind – but I really do think in this instance you are grasping at straws!

It is in no way unusual for people to use postcards, photographs, tissues, even Monopoly money, as bookmarks. I know for a fact that I once left a bay leaf as a marker in a recipe book – Page 267, Shanghai Dumplings - and on one occasion I bought a book from a local charity shop which had a deeply intimate letter stuffed between the last two pages. And a confession at that! I should add here that it is my deepest hope whoever wrote that missive is now resting at her Majesty's pleasure. Such filth! Anyway, the fact that you found this 'message', as you call it, should in no way surprise you. It's a perfectly run-of-the-mill occurrence and I exhort you not to read too much into it. I don't need to remind you that this is a bit of a well-worn path for you and is quite likely to end in tears. Again. Nonetheless, despite all my reservations, as you quite rightly say, we have been friends for a very long time, and as I value our friendship so highly I will do my best to respond to the points you have raised and to put your mind at rest.

You say that this all began when you asked the Universe for guidance on the matter of your relationship with you-know-who. My darling, why do you persist with that man? Have the past thirty years of marriage and continuous infidelities not been message enough? You know that if you had asked me, I would have told you in a very short sentence what you should do, but I'm aware that is not my place, so I will hold my peace on the matter. Except just to say that I had him pegged as a scoundrel the very day you introduced him to me. He was completely unable to look me straight in the eye and used far too much Brylcreem. But I digress. Back to your mysterious 'message'.

You say that the sign you received from the 'Universe' came to you through a news article in the Worthing Herald about the opening of the new library. I agree it's a lovely building in its own way, but I am still trying to fathom the very notion of a library with an ante-natal clinic.   There's modern and there's things that really are quite beyond me. Indeed, I wonder where all this modern will take us all next: funeral directors in the local leisure centre? Not the worst of ideas though, given that my doctor has taken to prescribing exercise instead of pills. The very idea. How on earth does a treadmill help my heart condition? My neighbour's doctor was far more sympathetic when she went to them with her varicose veins. But for some unearthly reason mine thinks the use of a rolling footpath to a noise that could never be described as music is the way forward. And as for the costume abominations you get in there. Whoever invented latex needs a very stern word. The treadmill is right next to the weight lifting section and at times I have had to avert my gaze by twisting my neck in a most unnatural manner. Anyway, I am going off on another tangent.

I agree it was very thoughtful of the young man who works at the library to offer you a tour. The fact his name was also Phillip (like you-know-who), and that he ended the tour in THAT particular section (Romantic Fiction) does seem like a bit of a coincidence. Myself, I would not have read too much into it, but as you say, you'd had a conversation with the Universe, so who's to argue. Personally, I can't even get a reply to the letter I sent to the Council about my rubbish bin, but hey-ho. Anyway, getting back to the note you found in the book, you say you believe this is far more than just a simple verse left at the beginning of the last chapter, with the reader intending to return and discover who indeed had done it. Rather, you believe that the first line has encoded within itself a clue to what the whole four-line verse is really about. Furthermore, you believe that you have had a moment of inspiration and realized that by taking the first letter of each word in the first line of the verse 'In search of true pleasure' - I S O T P - an anagram is revealed, an anagram of the word POSIT, and therefore, you contend, the first line explains the meaning of the entire poem. That is, it puts something forward as a fact or as a basis for argument.

I have to say, on reflection, that I would not have come to that conclusion immediately myself, but then

41

I was never any good at cryptic crosswords – something with which you have won prizes. Cash prizes, I seem to remember, which reminds me, darling, I paid for lunch last week, so maybe you wouldn't mind terribly obliging on Tuesday. And maybe we could try that little place on the seafront. Their menu is far more, shall we say, familiar than the place our last little foray took us to. So, as I say, I would maybe not initially have read quite so much into that simple opening line. However, the verse does indeed POSIT a point of view. And as I continued to follow the line of thought – that the first letter of each word might reveal an anagram – I found myself getting into something of a pickle, as follows:

Line 2 - HVWR

Line 3 - THIFL

Line 4 - WMFIAH

Well, first of all, I tried HVWR up, down, backwards and sideways, but you won't be surprised to hear it revealed absolutely nothing. I did have a little more luck with Line 3, which conceals an anagram of the word FILTH. I am reminded once again of the confessional note I found in the book from the charity shop. Clearly filth was someone's idea of true pleasure, but on that subject I'll say no more.

Regrettably, Line 4 - WMFIAH - also revealed nothing as an anagram. Does this mean that you are completely on the wrong track, I wondered? I do confess, at first, I thought so, but then, as I ruminated on the matter over a cup of tea and a slice of Sussex plum heavy, it occurred to me that the anagrams appeared in the first and third lines. But that, of course, could be another meaningless coincidence. Nonetheless, I know that I'm prone to being a tad judgemental – as you pointed out once on Brighton seafront following my comment about people down from London – so I am going to give the whole thing the benefit of the doubt and stick with my investigation into your mysterious message just as soon as I get back from taking my Jackapoo for his daily constitutional.

Darling, I had just returned home from walking my darling pooch when I had a visit from my niece. Such a smart girl. I think she takes after me. Doesn't resemble my sister in the slightest. Anyway, Veronica, my niece, told me about a place called google that you can go to, and it can come up with answers to every single question under the sun, quite the Oracle apparently, so I asked her if she could go and speak to the google and find out what HVWR might mean. Apparently, the google could only think of Hawaii Volcano Watch Reports. Not much help in Sussex, I would say. I then thought perhaps it might be Welsh, but my niece says no. She holidays regularly in Aberystwyth, so I didn't argue. I did start to fear that we were up a gum tree.

However, I then had the brainwave to phone Teddy. You remember Teddy. Quite the gentleman. Well, he went up to Cambridge as a youth. The University, not the town. Though of course, the University is in the town, but you get my meaning. Teddy's very interested in magical alphabets, so I gave him a tinkle and ran HVWR by him. He was absolutely intrigued. Says it sounded to him like a tetragrammaton. And what is one of those, I hear you say. My reaction exactly. I'd never heard of such a thing. Well, it seems they have a secret meaning. Very powerful ones as well, Teddy says. Apparently, there's a tetragrammaton over the west door in the King's College chapel. Teddy says it means something in Hebrew. I quite forget what. All funny handshakes if you ask me. Anyway, Teddy is going to investigate further and see what he can find out.

Forgetting anagrams for a minute, as it was getting me nowhere, I started to consider the possibility of *acronyms*. I can almost see you throwing your hands up in horror. An abuse of the English language and so adored by local government, I hear you shriek. But you started this wild goose chase, so just hear me out for a minute and consider the following:

WMFIAH - Worthing Maritime, Fishing Industry and Heritage.

Ta-dah! Hahaha. Yes. So simple. True pleasure right here under our very noses. As your message clearly states, we must find it at home. In our hometown. In our lifeblood. You know, I think I may be on to something. What do you think, darling? Oh dear, I'm feeling rather giddy. I must lie down and come back to this endeavour tomorrow. Exercise classes indeed. I knew my doctor should have given me tablets.

Darling, you are not going to believe what I am about to tell you. I was so very tired last night that I just downed tools, drank my Ovaltine, and made my way to my bed. I was asleep almost as soon as my head hit the pillow. I slept fitfully throughout the night but then awoke before five in the most dreadful tremble. I could remember only the remnants of my dream, but of one thing I'm sure – it concerns your verse. Before I slept, I had seen the lines as nothing more than a harmless aphorism. A few gentle words intended to guide, or to reassure. But this morning, with the grey light of the October dawn fingering the papers on my desk, the words seem to have taken on a completely new meaning. Whereas before I saw wisdom, I now see an ominous warning. In the innocent rhyme, a far darker purpose.

What, indeed, constitutes 'true pleasure'? The question has been going round and round in my head ever since I awoke. Suddenly, the enjoyable little walks along the seafront and elevenses in the tearooms have started to lose their meaning. They have taken on a quite superficial patina. I can hear Murray scratching at the door, wanting his morning walkies. But should I be attending to a higher purpose? My mind is all a flutter.

And what of 'To hold it for life'. What yesterday had seemed a path to eternal peace of mind and happiness, I am now seeing in a completely different light. Hold on to life, it says. Hold on to life before it slips through your bony fingers. Before it flies away like a bird. Does life fly like a bird? Is that what it is saying? But worse, far worse, and the core of my sleep's dark mare, is the imperative that the answer must be found, and that we must find it at home. In my dream, I am searching

45

throughout my house. I pull open cupboards and drawers, old suitcases, bags I had forgotten I owned. I climb into the loft. Spider webs cling to my hair as I fumble my way through the cast off detritus of my past. But for what am I looking? I am searching in vain, I am vainly searching, but with the dread feeling that if I do not find it then a terrible fate will befall me. I have been awake for hours now, but I cannot shake the feeling. I retain the sense that I must continue to search in this very house for an answer. Or I am doomed.

Darling, what a chump you must believe I am. How a disturbed sleep can rattle the sharpest of brains. But I am happy to report that after my breakfast I dozed on my old horsehair chaise, the one by the window overlooking the sea, and I have awoken feeling quite refreshed. Teddy has just phoned and quite put my mind at rest. He has perused his books of magical alphabets and can find absolutely no sinister explanation for HVWR, not even using something called *gematria*. No, I'd never heard of it before either. Something to do with numbers, letters, and codes. Quite ancient, Teddy says. He's quite happy to have a chat with you at some time about his research. In fact, I had to make an excuse that the postman was at the door just to bring the phone call to an end, so enthusiastic is he about the subject.

You know, darling, I think we should just see your mysterious message as that POSIT you found in the first line. Has the Universe given you the answer you sought? As one of your oldest friends I would say that the only thing that matters is your peace of mind. A mystery is all very well, but best kept between the covers of a good book, don't you think? If we learnt anything from that day in Eastbourne, it is not to look too deeply into matters. Just tell yourself that the message was left by an unknown reader and that although there was never any intent, the words on the piece of paper used as a bookmark were nothing more than a sweet jotting of wisdom. As for Phillip, well, just put him right out of your mind. Are we still on for elevenses on Wednesday?

Darling, another night of broken sleep, rent through with dreams of searching. High and low. Low and high. And with such a sense of dread. The dream gives me nothing of what I am searching for, but I know for sure that if I do not find it, something awful will happen. Teddy phoned again to say that he has discovered something else in your message. Truly, I wanted to tell him that I have no interest, that he should take his findings straight to you. It was, after all, you who approached the Universe in the first place with your question.

I know I went to the google, well, not me directly, but through my niece, but I was not seeking an answer for myself. So why am I now being so plagued? It is coming to the point where I fear closing my eyes, for it brings back the same sense of dread. And even with my eyes open, I am driven by a notion that I should be searching. It is Eastbourne, darling. Eastbourne all over again. The carved initials on the bench. You-know-who's initials. In a heart. I only pointed out the coincidence that they were his initials, but you became so convinced it was further evidence of P's infidelity. I should have dismissed it on sight. There are, after all, only twenty-six letters in the alphabet. Yes, there are a seemingly infinite number of combinations, and PQS are perhaps unique and unusual – how many people have Quentin as a middle name – but for all we knew, it was just a coincidence. There was no need to go to the lengths of a private investigator. Such a seedy profession. And what was the outcome of all the expense? Only confirmation of what I could have told you myself. The man is a philanderer, and you are better off without him. Did you really need the Universe to confirm it? And in such a perverse way? Heaven knows, It is already the modern way to read far too much into every word. For the sake of peace, can we not just see a word for what it does? How I long for the simplicity of the child's classroom. Do you remember, darling? Old Miss Proops? A noun is a naming word. A verb is a doing word. That's all we need in life, isn't it darling? Just naming and doing. So simple. All this meaning upon meaning.

No wonder there is so much conflict in the world. We can barely speak plainly to each other anymore. I know you say I speak too plainly at times – you told me that time we had an altercation at the railway station. But I had a very good point. Using apostrophes were there should be letters, or worse, abbreviating names like they are no longer fashionable is bound to end with some poor soul heading for Sou and ending up in Sef. Sorry, darling, I must go now – I can hear Teddy coming up the path – but I will get straight back to you when he leaves. I wonder what it is he has found?

Darling, forgive me for my non-arrival at our cake and coffee rendezvous. You know I have never let you down before and if I leave my hospital bed alive and well, I will never let you down again. The doctor says it was not my heart as they at first feared, but a panic attack. A panic attack! I have never heard the like. Is this an actual condition, I asked them? Conditions come and go, as we who have been on this earth for so many decades could tell the youngsters like the hospital registrar who dealt with me. Whoever hears of catatonia anymore? It has gone quite out of favour now. But when I was a girl it was surprisingly common. And we didn't have such a thing as an eating disorder. We had rationing. Anyway, suffice to say I have been prescribed meditation classes which they say will help me with my over-breathing. What they do not know, and I shall never tell them, is the cause of the onset of my acute condition.

It was Teddy's finding. Something we had all missed in our fixation with the verse and the possibility of some hidden meaning.

Hidden meaning! Ha. Had we just thought to turn the note over. To look on the other side. Then we would have seen it. The clue.

Teddy now says it is clear evidence the note is code, and that you may be on to something. I believe he may

49

be right. And I hope that is the answer. I really do. I tell myself that it is my dream that has no meaning. It is all part of the panic. And in any case, the message was not meant for Teddy. Or me. It was meant for you. And it may well be the Universe has spoken. I am just hoping that I will leave the hospital soon, and return to a more peaceful life, with no confusions or mysteries. I so long for the simplicity we once knew. Before things became so complicated. Oh, that reminds me. Teddy is going have a quiet word with someone he knows who enjoys conundrums. In the meantime, darling, I will leave you with the words he found on the back of your message.

'The bird has flown'.

5
Graham Knapman

What does a published playwright do on a wet Saturday afternoon?

This isn't a rhetorical question.

My routine has kind of evolved over the years. I enjoy making bread. So, on Saturdays, I make pizza.

Last Saturday was different. Something a little out of the ordinary happened, which meant that I ended up with sir fried mince.

I was standing at my lounge window watching the rain falling on my neighbour's paving stones. I don't normally do that, but she had recently bought a pressure washer: and I was wondering if she thought it had been worthwhile.

It was best if I let her bring the subject up.

Anyway, I have a flat on the first floor. I fell in love with the place within minutes of seeing it. It's manageable. Some people would dismiss it out of hand for being too small, but I love it.

There is a builders merchant at the end of the garden. I only mention this because you can't miss it. Luckily, there are several large trees which hide the view in the Summer.

On a more positive note, the Co-op is at the end of

the road.

My downstairs neighbour is called Alice. I wouldn't mind betting that she got her paving stones when they were on special offer in the builders merchant. And she is one of those people who knows everything. She could probably write a book about the house going back to when it was built in the 1930s.

To most people it's a red brick semi.

If you listen to local policians you will hear a lot about the Lancing Gap, or Goring Gap. These terms are used to describe green spaces which were left between former villages.

These gaps have shrunk over the years, and are linked together by the A259.

In the 1920's there were a few fisherman's cottages along Ham Road. The B2223 is now a rat run from Brighton Road to The Range.

I've seen photographs of Worthing from the Edwardian period which show country lanes instead of trunk roads.

If you followed the Brighton Road East as far as Southwick in 1915 you would have found an army camp on The Green. I know because I used to live in Southwick.

Alice is very keen on her garden: and I helped her to bring a neglected corner of it back to life. I had always liked the idea of gardening. It was the actual work I wasn't so keen on, but we managed.

We laid gravel, and created a rockery.

There was something on television about birdwatching. I thought it was good idea to get a birdfeeder. And Alice agreed. I hung the birdfeeder on a stake so that I could see it from my window.

A few weeks later I happened to mention that the pigeons were very well fed. 'You shouldn't feed them in the Summer', came her sage advice.

So I stopped.

It goes without saying that the sparrows had created an awful mess.

Alice is a vegan so I didn't tell her that I had eaten pigeon in the Lake District. Nor did I mention my answer to the seagull problem.

The fact is that I haven't been able to take pigeons seriously since Mel Brooks took a swipe at them in a couple of his films. The Produces with Zero Mostel and Gene Wilder is a classic. High Anxiety isn't bad either.

Last Saturday I thought about putting the heating on again. I saw the birdfeeder hanging on its ornamental stake so I went out and bought some more food.

In the afternoon I saw this pigeon. It was larger than the pigeons I had seen before, and it had a very long neck.

There was a message attached to its leg.

Carrier pigeons are descended from the rock dove: and I read somewhere that they bought news of Napoleon's defeat at Waterloo.

Worthing was a small fishing village back then.

One hundred years later carrier pigeons were still being used to bring news from the trenches. What was a pigeon doing with a message tied to its leg in 2021?

I had no idea.

So I googled.

The Swiss Army didn't disband their pigeon until

1996.

While India still suspect Pakistan of using pigeons as a means of spying.

Worthing is a long way from Pakistan.

The pigeon didn't seem to be interested in food so I went downstairs for a closer look.

I used to be able to transfer our pet budgerigar from the floor back to its cage. Pigeons are just a bit bigger: and it didn't seem to mind.

I had expected the message to be in trench code, but it wasn't. It was a poem in plain English:

In search of true pleasure

How vainly we roam.

To hold it for life

We must find it at home.

There was another line, but I couldn't read it. The paper had got wet.

The words I had read were familiar.

I vaguely remember having seen the legend on a plaque outside a cottage in Warwick Place. It was a few years ago now. I had only just moved here from Southwick, and I was curious.

Warwick Place is a row of cottages dating back some two hundred years. The plaque had appeared to be weather worn so there was a good chance that it was an original feature.

I didn't take a great deal of notice of the poem, but I came across it again in *The London Magazine* when I was researching my family history. The magazine dated from 1747. The poem itself was anonymous.

Typing the first line of a poem into Google will normally reveal the name of the poet. In search of true pleasure . . .

And there it was.

Still anonymous.

A link to Facebook told me that the plaque had been sold for twenty quid a couple of years ago by a local dealer. An additional message claimed that a shop in Lancing used to sell verse plaques.

Upon further reflection I had seen similar plaques on sale in garden centres and gift shops. They are also very popular across The Pond. My Canadian cousins have them in their gardens.

I emailed them.

Did I know the author of the poem?

It's anonymous.

Traditional.

Yes.

Nothing wrong with traditional.

No.

When are you coming back to Toronto?

Who says that the art of conversation is dead?

I used to do market stalls. One year we had a glut of plastic gravestones from China. Some of those had poems on them.

Back in the day Dennis Potter wrote a play for television called *Brimstone and Treacle*. Denholm Elliott played a man who earned his living from writing religious verse. Sting was what one might call an avenging angel.

The BBC refused to screen it.

I saw it at the cinema.

I wasn't a market trader for long. People think that they are getting bargains. They aren't. A new generation is discovering Only Fools and Horses on Gold.

In search of true pleasure

How vainly we roam.

To hold it for life

We must find it at home.

I was tempted to show the poem to Alice, but I suspect that she would have dismissed it as trite rubbish.

I began thinking about similar poems which extol the virtues of home. I couldn't recite them but titles, and odd phrases, came readily to mind.

There's no place like home.

I googled it.

John Howard Payne

Too long from the fireside you roam.

Mary Tarver Carroll

And Home makes one's happiness complete was by Eliza Wolcott.

Does anyone remember these people?

I certainly don't.

According to the internet, Home Sweet Home became an anthem for soldiers during the American Civil War.

What I didn't understand was how this 'thing' came to be wrapped round the leg of a pigeon in my garden.

It was then that I had a bit of a funny turn. Warwick Place is few hundred yards from Beach House Park here in Worthing. The council put up a memorial to those who died at the Battle of Boars Head which was fought in France the summer of 1916.

The Royal Sussex Regiment had suffered a great

many losses there

Further investigation revealed that pigeons were awarded the Dickin Medal in World War One.

I was struck by the idea of a soldier in the trenches having this message typed out for him on a battered Underwood, and attaching it to the leg of a pigeon so that it might find its way back to England.

My pigeon was swinging on the birdfeeder. So I took hold of it and put the message back in the little canister, and went back upstairs to make my pizza.

I bake from scratch because I'm lactose intolerant. I don't have tomatoes either because they cause heartburn. Salmon and mushroom pizza is fine. It's a weekend treat because it does twice.

I looked out of my lounge window just in time to see the pigeon fly off.

6

Heather Gosling

It was the middle of Summer. Clara stood at the edge of the pier looking out. Listening to the sound of the sea made her feel alive. She felt every ripple of every wave, every cloud that partially obscured the melting sun, she soaked it all up before it all drifted from her fingertips. She had achieved her dream of becoming a teacher, today she finished teaching her third class of the term. Then, she heard the news. The nurse's lips moved but she must have become deaf because the words did not reach her ears. But she knew. She knew that something was not right, and that nothing could be done. What would she tell her kids? She couldn't bear the thought of a strange new teacher entering her classroom.

Her body felt heavy, and questions spiralled through her mind. If only there was a way to avoid the inevitable, to hide oneself from the eyes of Death. A seagull flew over Clara's head, dropping a piece of parchment as it went. Clara picked it up, turning it over in her hands.

"In search of true pleasure
How vainly we roam

To hold it for life
We must find it at home
The bird has flown."

Clara stood, puzzled. She folded up the paper and put it in her jean pocket.

The next morning, Clara visited *Time,* her usual cafe spot. The walls were painted terracotta orange, paintings and antique clocks hung from the walls.

"Your usual?" Theo asked.

"Yes, please"

When she looked at him, the whole world reduced to that room. Theo had one of those rare, genuine smiles that transfixed you, held you at your spot and made you feel important. She loved the time they spent together, and her heart clenched at the thought of that being taken away. She wanted to tell him about her diagnosis, but it was never the right time.

Theo switched on the coffee machine and began his ritualistic actions of making her a cup of coffee. "So, I have some news." He said.

"Me too." She had to tell him.

"Well, you go first."

"No, no. You go."

"I'm buying the cafe. The owner wanted to put it on the market, so I expressed my interest. He accepted my offer, now this place is mine." Theo looked triumphantly around at the cafe's interior.

"That's incredible Theo."

"What was your news?"

"Well, I found this poem on the pier." Clara fished the poem out from her pocket. She would have to tell him another day. "What do you think it means?"

Theo read the poem closely. "I recognise this symbol," he said, pointing to the ink stamp of the bird. "The bird is a Phoenix. Like the one on your locket. It's a symbol of immortality"

Clara touched her locket. "What about the rest of the poem?"

"I wouldn't think too much about it. Maybe it's a love poem written by some love struck teenager."

"I've got to dash, but thank you." Theo hugged Clara goodbye. She left the cafe, her red hair shining in the sun. The poem still buried its way in the labyrinth of her mind.. There was something she had to do.

Clara stood outside her Father's house, staring at the brass door knocker, afraid to knock. She needed her Dad now more than ever, and she needed to tell him the truth. The door opened. He stood in the doorway in his striped dressing gown that had holes in the armpits. His fingernails were painted dark blue to match his glasses. He had always been an eccentric man, preferring to study from books than interact with people.

"What are you doing lurking out here? Come in." He waved for her to come up the steps.

They walked through a formal, dark hallway, passed a gothic staircase and entered the lounge. Clara nearly tripped over piles of precariously stacked books placed in her path.

They sat and drank tea in silence.

"How is work coming along?" Clara asked.

"Everyone at the lab thinks I'm crazy. No one will give me any funding because apparently dark matter is a lost cause." Clara's Father looked down at his feet.

"I'm sorry to hear that, Dad. I think your research is brilliant."

"What do you think of this?" Clara passed the poem.

"Who sent you this?"

"A seagull dropped it on me while I was on the pier. I don't know who wrote it."

"What did the seagull look like?"

Clara frowned, confused at the implied significance of the seagull. "He had black tipped wings."

"That's Bertie. He is a dear, old friend of mine. He visits every morning. Bertie sent me a message as well."

He showed Clara the message that read: "Find Clara. Pass on her message."

Clara watched as her Dad leant over the poem reading it slowly word for word.

"So what is your true pleasure Clara? What would make you happy?"

Clara felt her lip wobble. Her eyes filled with water. The whole room went blurry.

"I just don't want to die."

She felt a hand on her shoulder.

"The bird has flown. Everything will be alright. Trust me. The message needs to find everyone, and fast. There is a reason you have been given this message, Clara. Everything is connected. You, me, the

61

trees, the sea, the stars and all the people out there. All connected. Someone must know the true meaning of this message, we need to find them."

"I don't have long left," Clara said.

"I think sending this message is our duty, by fulfilling our duty the universe will reward us. There is a greater meaning behind all of this, I'm sure of it. If we send this message, you will be reborn."

"How do we send the message?" Clara asked.

She watched her Dad pace up and down the lounge. Then, he stopped.

"By water. When the moon is at its fullest."

Clara stood on the pier, watching the moonlight turn the waves silver. She looked up at the moon, hoping that she could trust it to send the message to its rightful recipient. She placed the poem into her locket and dropped it off the side of the pier. It made a small splash, and sank into the darkness of the Ocean, carrying her message across countries, continents and time itself.

She awoke to the sound of clocks ticking. She felt her lungs. There was no more pain. Her mind recalled last night. The last moment she remembered was standing at the edge of the pier, hoping that by sending the message on, she could live. She made her hands into fists and wriggled her toes, just to make sure. Yes, she was here. Alive. She looked around. This was *Time*, and she was lying on the sofa next to the till. Theo was busy serving customers, and greeting them with his smile. He walked over and kissed her forehead. Clara closed her eyes. Now, she was at peace. She had been reborn.

The message was out there for others to discover.

7
Kayleigh Ackerman

Midnight. Bells adorning stone roofs ring to announce the start of another year. Housewives and servants in every home have swept old ash from the hearth, clearing space for whatever blessings the new year will bring. Drowned by the sound of the bells is a shout of *Welcome!* from various door frames, families silhouetted against the warm firelight from within. The heat of their voices leaves smoke trails that rise and join with the warmth of a thousand chimneys in the frosty London air.

As the bells tire of their song and the time ticks on into early morning, the patchwork of lit windows on a neat row of houses are gradually extinguished. One remains lit even as the bells signal that an hour has passed, then two. Long after other souls are tucked up in bed dreaming of Eggnog and dancing. Even as the lamplighters bounce around from light to light in the brightening streets and girls prepare for their society debut, giggling nervously in the pale dawn. Even then, the light has not gone out.

In that window is the darkened shape of a woman. She is seated at a mahogany desk, writing in a small leather-bound journal. Her script is a dense mass of curved letters, swirling into one another and leaning over as though they'd indulged themselves too much at the New Year dance. She has written:

London, 1824, 1-

The rest of the page stares accusingly back at her. Since childhood she has written a journal, but she has never – until now – considered why. It occurred to her that she had begun writing because she knew her mother had, or perhaps to process the loss of her. At some point she supposed that she was writing only for prosperity, to maintain a record in case history should mind her life. The final thought, the one which stopped her progressing further than the date, was that she had been writing the diary for her children.

As the first of her neighbours advance into the snow-soaked paths, stamping cold feet and breathing into their hands, the woman stands. Slowly, with one hand, she closes her journal and vanishes into the darkness of the hall. She is alone in the house. For all that she cares, she could be alone in all the world. The muffled shouts of children pelting snowballs permeate her walls, but she does not hear them. She is hearing other children, ones who could have grown to build snowmen with bold carrot noses, who would have stolen their father's hat to make their snowperson a gentleman. She is thinking of three little boys with thick coats and scarves giggling and squealing as they race down a white mountain on their sledge.

She prepares some food from the pantry and carries it on a tray into the back parlour where a small fire crackles lazily in the grate. She remembers her father and stepmother producing daintily wrapped parcels with brightly coloured ribbons from behind their backs and bestowing them. Pictures her father's smiling face as he hands her candy, the phantom of a sugared mouse dissolves on her tongue as she thinks back. Most of all she remembers sitting in the shadows in the corner of the room watching her half siblings open their gifts, waiting for someone to realise she was still there.

The first year after her marriage, New Year was spent dancing and dreaming to the music in their heads, while the pleasure of their own company was still enough. This fizzled out quickly. Future years were spent flitting from house to house, visiting various friends for extravagant buffets, exchanging gifts and laughing at the young couples flirting on the periphery.

Today she has no plans. Almost everybody she knows is holding an open house and she has of course been invited, but she cannot imagine herself walking outside of this house. Inside this space she can imagine that everything is as she dreams, that if she were to step outside she would find her children laughing and pushing in the snow, her husband watching over them, glass in hand and gossiping with a neighbour. If she leaves the house she will have to encounter reality and so she remains inside, even as she knows that to do so on the first day of the year is to bring upon herself a year of perpetual loneliness.

A while later, when she reaches for her plate and finds only crumbs, she ventures back upstairs with the thought that she will try again with the journal. Winter has enforced an early evening and the silent darkness stretches out around her, the little candle burning in her hand barely cutting a path through the inky black of the empty house. She reaches the study and the darkness is banished to the corners as she reawakens the fire dozing in the grate. Lighting the lamp on the desk, she settles back into her chair and watches the snow falling onto sleepy streets. Pauses before opening her diary. She lifts the journal and holds it closer to the lamp for scrutiny, rubs her eyes and looks again. Clear, neat letters stand to attention on the page beneath her lilting record of the date.

London, 1824, 1-
In search of true pleasure,
　　how vainly we roam,
　　to hold it for life,
we must find it at home.

Placing the diary carefully back on the desk, she looks into the darkness beyond the study door. She holds her breath and listens. There is nothing. A sudden gust of wind makes the window rattle and she jumps backwards, knocking her chair into the desk. *Foolish fanciful woman.* There must be a simple explanation: a servant home early from the festivities, or simply a tired mind perhaps. She takes the candle up again and begins lighting the lamps down the hall, shouting for the servants and then pausing to listen for a response. Soon she has swept the entire house and found no evidence of another's presence. A friend must have snuck in while she'd been eating downstairs. Silently. They were sly as a fox to come through her front door without making a sound and to avoid the sixth step, which always creaks. What a cruel joke. Mischief in return for one of the declined invitations perhaps.

She hastens back upstairs, extinguishing candles as she goes until she reaches her bedroom. The room is dominated by a four-post bed, luxurious blood-red fabric tied neatly to the sides and revealing clean cotton bedsheets. This bed was not hers originally, sometimes while she lies abed her mind strays to thoughts of those who have lain there before her and she is struck by the weight of their presence. She wonders how they died: whether it was quick and peaceful; or whether, like much of the death she has known, it was sudden and sharp.

Settling at her dressing table she ponders the words in the note. *In search of true pleasure, how vainly we roam.* In her life that has always proved true, with joy being elusive and once gained, short. A search in vain, guaranteeing more pain than pleasure. The alignment of her own views with the note leaves her considering that she may have written the note herself and forgotten in her exhaustion. She feels calmed by this. After brushing her hair and using the chamber pot, she climbs between the comfort of her sheets, leaving the curtains open to allow warmth from the fireplace to reach her as she sleeps.

An icy draft wakes her and she shoots upright in bed. Heart racing, her eyes dart around in the darkness, trying to catch sight of something. She realises that she has been looking for the monster she created and shakes her head, smirking at her own foolishness. She is struck by the memory of a long ago visit to Bethlem Hospital and the women there talking to beings she could not see. She will not allow things to make her hysterical, there is always a rational explanation. At some point the window has blown open and the cold wind is leading the curtains in a manic dance. Reluctantly, she wraps the sheet around herself and crosses the room to drag the sash down.

Despite her best attempts to control her nerves, when she returns to bed, she finds herself unable to sleep and is soon informed by the bells of St Michael's Church that it is four hours after midnight. That will suffice, the first light of day is still a long way off, but she has always been early to rise. She washes in the cold water that sits upon her dresser, changes into fresh clothes for the first time this year and heads to find herself something to eat.

She will stay inside again today: the finding of that note has bothered her more than she would like to admit and knowing that this is silly makes it no easier to get control of herself. Even as she is thinking this, she is distracted by wondering why in this world someone would suggest that one could find pleasure at home. She wonders who wrote it initially, whether it is some extract from a poet she is yet to read or if it is an original work. Of whose? She sighs, that is a question best avoided. In any case she certainly wouldn't have considered home to be the source of any good thing.

She has always felt herself to be an afterthought at

home, perhaps after years of being second or third or fourth to preferred siblings. Or a by-product of living life in the shadows of the infamous mother she never had the chance to know. Her home had been the smallest room at the back of the house with a view that only had a view of roof-tiles. She was the last to be served at dinner and the first to be sent to her bedroom afterwards. Unlike her half-sister, interruptions while the adults were talking were not sweet, but intolerable. Occasionally she was invited to join in games with her siblings, but this was after everybody else had been asked and only to fill the roles in make believe that they hadn't wanted.

As an adult, her home has become a museum of lost hopes. Here she is haunted by images of children sprawled across the back parlour, playing with a dolls house or little wooden animals. Dreams of reading stories to little ones all tucked up in their little beds, comforting them after a nightmare. She had projected herself forward in those days, imagined a life in which she had grown old, hair greying, wrinkled hands holding her husband's in the firelight. All these other versions of her live on in the house, she can almost hear their voices, it is a constant torment.

Home is loneliness, isolation, pain.

Again, she thinks of her monster, though this time it is without fear. She thinks of his longing for love and acceptance. He longs, really, for the happy ending he can never have. She feels a pinch of guilt, but she could not have given him the ending he deserves. *Why?* She reflects on her own life, of the happiness she wanted but has never found and realises that she could not give him an ending happier than her own.

This makes her laugh. It is a laugh without humour: dry; short; ended with a sigh. Is it madness that she sees this as her ending at twenty-five years of age? She knows many who lost their lives much earlier than this, it is good fortune to survive even for another day in this city. Is she doomed to the same tragic ending of this fearsome, unnatural creature?

She wonders where the monster would place his home. Would it be in the halls of Victor's home? The place where he was birthed? Perhaps not, perhaps his lack of a home was the reason he tried to find home in people. Without this fanciful notion would we just be happy as we were, without searching so desperately?

The stillness of the air before dawn softens and gives way to a burst of bird song and the crunch of wheels on roads as men make their way to work, caps pulled down and collars up against the frozen January air. A door slams in one of the houses nearby and she hears someone holler at the noise.

This is the problem with London these days, so many people crammed into the space that there's no peace and yet there's no solace in the closeness of the neighbours. She thinks she could die in here all alone and nobody would know until she started to smell. She supposes that these are the kind of thoughts that earn you a place in the asylum, but somehow can't get away from them. There's nobody alive to complete the paperwork for her in any case so she'll be safe for now.

She thinks she might have dozed off, because the

71

fire is sleeping in the grate and there's a new chill in the air. She considers lighting it again but can't bring herself to move. Thoughts of the note still crowd her mind, she sits back further in the chair and considers alternatives to the notes' suggestion. She has never found happiness at home, but has she found it elsewhere? There was pleasure on her wedding day, the excitement of stealing away with the love of her life, she had been entirely caught up in the passion and daring of it all. Of course, the publication of her novel brought her pride, a great sense of having succeeded where others had failed, where others thought she might fail too. Most precious was the momentary joy of holding her child before life stole him away. All this happiness, captured in the moment and then lost, remaining only in a snow globe of memory.

Is this the intention of the note? She still has no memory of writing it and even in a tired state does not believe she would have forgotten. There has been no occasion previously during which she considered writing poetry and to try while so fatigued would have been lunacy. Her father was a poet, but she finds no solace in this link. The room is dimly lit by daylight leaking in at the windows. Her breath is visible, lingering in the frosty air as she asks: *Are you my monster?* She holds her breath, half expecting the dead silence to answer. Nothing stirs.

She allows herself to think the word she's been avoiding. *Ghost.* She writes about these things, but never for a second paused to believe it. Could it be true? Shivering, she pulls her shawl more tightly around her shoulders and thinks of all the people she has lost. Death has been a truer companion to her than any. Drowning, poison, suicide. The Grim Reaper has always stalked her life: taking her mother, siblings, children, husband. Even as the harbinger of death and bad fortune she feels he may be her closest companion. Her only companion perhaps, even as her monster mourned the loss of his detested creator, she feels she would rather have Death accompanying her than nobody.

Once again, she feels a tugging toward the wretch who had been created to be beautiful. She sees his thin yellow skin and watery eyes, the shrivelled face and dead black lips. She sees the hurt in his eyes as he is tortured by all those who encounter him. It was her who did all these things to him. With her pen she had ensured that his features combined to produce such a monstrosity, that nobody would take pity on him. She forced him to live without love. Without joy.

Joy is not to be found where he searched for it and, having crafted the ending, she feels she should have realised this sooner. It is insanity to continue in the same course of action despite knowing that it will not work, and from the example of this poor creature's life it should have been evident that there was no home to be found in others. There is no home in the past, in raising lost loves, or in living amid broken dreams. As she thinks these things there is a growing sense of excitement within her and she wonders if perhaps she has finally lost the last of her sanity, locked up in this house alone. She has clung for too long to the hopes of times past. She will have to create a place for herself in the world, make a home for herself that does not stand on the love of others.

In a burst of energy, she springs from her seat and hurries up the stairs without pausing to pick up a candle. The winter sun filters through the new snow that falls outside the window, illuminating the study in silver light. She sits back in the chair where she spent New Year's Eve and picks up the pen from where she had dropped it. Gently, she opens the journal to the first page, ready to record something. Not in memory of her mother or for her children or for prosperity anymore, but for herself. To remind her in the days and weeks and years to come that she is enough. That she does not need to rely on those around her to be her home or her joy, that she can be that for herself.

She says goodbye. Goodbye to the ghosts of those she has lost, to the ghosts of her broken dreams and the memories that have haunted her. The relief at leaving these things is so palpable that she almost waves at them, and then with a deep breath she lowers her gaze to the journal.

London, 1824, 1-
In search of true pleasure,
    How vainly we roam,
    To hold it for life,
We must find it at home.

London, 1824, 2-
    The bird has flown.

8

Kate Morrison

Someone was talking to her. They had a high, clear, voice; a child's voice, and they were repeating the same words over and over again. The noise made her head throb.

"Home," said the child, "Home, home. Hold it for life. Find it at home. "

"Shh," said Anna. Was it Christmas morning? There were always children waking her too early on Christmas morning, at Lizzie's house. Nieces and nephews, bouncing up onto the bed with their stockings, squealing.

"Hold it for life. Hold, hold," said the child, louder now.

"For fuck's sake," said Anna. "Go and find Lizzie. It's too early."

"Hold," said the child, and then it placed a hand on her arm. The hand was so cold, as cold as the dark water in deep caves, that she sat up in fright and opened her eyes. The darkness did not lighten one iota. She strained her eyes, scanning to see the child that had left so freezing a touch on her skin, but still she could see nothing.

"Rose?" she whispered. "Ellie?"

"Home," the child whispered back, and in the darkness, Anna scrabbled away from the sound of its voice until her back hit rock and she could go no further. The sound of her breath in the darkness was terrifying, her own fear gasping back at her. There was very little echo: she was in a small space. A small space, made of rock.

Yes, the rock was familiar. She had been here when she fell asleep, but something had been different. The sound. The wind and rain. The scream of the wind above her head; a monstrous scream unlike anything she had ever heard before, had gone. It was silent in the cave apart from her own breath. But she had been alone when she passed out, for certain. No children. The children were long gone.

She let out a long breath, and the pain in her head throbbed again. She put a hand to it, and felt a strange, textured strip running over her hair. There was no feeling in it. Something had warped her skin and killed the feeling.

"Oh god, oh god," she said aloud, feeling up and down it, desperate for any sensation, until her fingers reached her forehead and found a protuberance: a small, solid, square, lump, sticking out at the front.

"Oh," she said again, as her fingers reached a round button. "Oh, you fuckwit."

She pressed the button on the head-torch and a weak beam of light shone out. The battery was dying, but in the light she could see the walls of white chalk, her own outstretched legs in blue trousers and walking boots, covered in chalky smears, and the child.

When she saw the child she froze, pushing her back

hard against the rock behind her as if it could protect her somehow. It was an impossible sight: a little girl, sitting cross legged on the floor. Her hair was braided and she was wearing some kind of tunic, one of those things made of flax or hemp or rough cotton that Lizzie and her friends favoured for their children, all natural look and slub and earth colours.

She was looking right at Anna with eyes that shone silver in the blanched light of the torch. Her feet were bare and calloused, her legs caked with dirt up to the knee.

"Home," said the girl in her clear voice, and she raised up her hand, holding the palm out towards Anna. "Hold it for life. Find it at home."

With her arm still extended, she moved it to her right, until her palm pressed against the wall of rock.

"Hold," she said, and her calm voice became more insistent, almost pleading. "*Home*. The bird is flown."

She looked towards her hand, and Anna turned her head to follow her gaze. As she moved, the torch flickered off. When it came on again two seconds later, the girl was gone. Anna moved her head from side to side, wildly, hunting for her. The space was only a couple of metres long, and a metre wide. Rock entombed them. The narrow slit that led out of the space was so positioned that there was no way the girl could have wriggled into it and out of the space in the two seconds the torch had been off.

Shakily, Anna crawled on hands and knees to the place where the girl had been. There. She had been there. Her palm had rested on that flat span of rock, just above a place where the chalk jutted out. The beam of the torch flashed over the wall, and something moved there. Gritting her teeth, Anna shone the torch onto it, full beam, and saw it was not a living thing but a little carving. Shallow lines, carved into the rock. Wings, tail, a curved beak. A bird of prey – a kestrel, a sparrowhawk. She put out her hand and felt the grooves, the shape of the creature.

"The bird is flown."

Were they extinct now, kestrels? It was hard to keep track. Whoever carved this bird must have known the shape intimately. Perhaps when it was made, the sky was full of kestrels, treading water in the sky, eyes fixed on the grass below them and the little lives scampering through it. Imagine lying on the hill, watching them hunt. Taking in the fluid, predator's line of their body. Anna traced it now with her fingers. Hold. Home. The bird is flown.

The torch went out again and she swore, shaking her head to try and revive it. This time, it stayed off. For a moment, in the darkness, she panicked. What if the girl came back? What if she was sitting there again, watching?

She sobbed in fear, tried to pull herself together. Then, as her eyes became used to the darkness, she saw it was not quite pitch black any longer. There was a very faint ribbon of light against the back wall, at the spot where the crack opened out into the mineshaft beyond. The night was over: the sun was rising. She was alive.

Shivering, she began to crawl towards the light, bumping past the now-empty bottle of Talisker she had brought down with her. That explained the head.

78

Perhaps it explained the girl too, but it could not explain the bird. Her small rucksack was still on her back. She must have properly blacked out. As she squeezed through the narrow passage back to the mineshaft, she recalled coming through on the way down. The rising wind. The long white breakers on the sea.

At the bottom of the shaft, she lifted her head to the light. Pale, grudging light, but still – it was the sun. The sun was still here. Slowly, hand over hand, she climbed back up the shaft using the cracks and shelves left by the excavations, until she came up over the top and onto the short turf of the Ring.

She lay there for a moment, back on the warm turf, staring up at the sky. It was blue, with shreds of cloud hurrying overhead. There was a breeze still, stirring the gorse bushes around her, but it was gentle. A mere echo of last night's horror. She knew she must move soon, and look at the rest of the world, but just for a few minutes she stayed there, breathing in the coconut-honey smell of the yellow gorse flowers and the green smell of the grass. Something tickled her hand and she peered down to see an ant crawling over her fingers, hurrying on its way. So the ants were still here too. The gorse flowers and the ants were here, and the sun, and so was she.

She sat up and pushed herself up onto wobbly legs, keeping her eyes on the ground as she made her way out of the gorse and towards the lower ramparts of the Ring. She would not look round until she was at the top. Looking down at her boots, she went step by step up the ancient earthworks until she stood on the brow

79

of the Ring. Now she could not avoid it any longer. Slowly she turned round, and looked down at the valley below her.

Water filled the whole valley and the flat land beyond. She followed the shine of it in utter disbelief, from the deep lake before her, south to where the town used to meet the sea. There was a break; a line of land, between the water and the sea, but there was no town any more. There were no houses any more, at all.

The long sprawl of suburb that had ranged along the valley floor was submerged. The valley formed by a glacier, many thousands of years ago, had been filled again. Yesterday, when she prepared to go down into the earth, the houses of the town had still been there. Many of them empty and abandoned, but still standing. In recent years the sea had encroached, had swallowed first one line of homes and then another, greedily marching onward towards the Downs, but there had still been enough left of the town to call it a town.

Now it was gone, in one gulp. The monster storm and the sea had conspired together and swallowed it, ironed it out. Somewhere beneath the water was Anna's house. Somewhere just there, near the line of land before the sea. Her house, her things. Her piano. All her clothes. The things she had kept, stupidly, because although there was no point and nothing made anything better, they still reminded her of her old life. The mug with a badly drawn Christmas tree on, from Rose. A bottle of Lizzie's perfume. A stack of birthday and Christmas cards filled with childish handwriting. Gone.

She sat down on the grass and stared, for a long time. Then, stung by a memory, she pulled the rucksack from her back and scrabbled in it, hunting for her phone. It was dead. No charge. Passing out drunk on whisky, remembering to turn off her phone had been the last thing on her mind. There had been endless warnings yesterday, from the one remaining Emergency Department, beeping out reminders to take shelter. No-one came in person any more, to the coastal towns and villages. Everyone had been warned, long ago, and there were far too many other things to be dealing with. Surely this might prompt a rescue party, though? Surely they would send out a helicopter to survey and record the damage?

She twisted round and stared up at the top of the hill, and saw that things were different there too. Trees strewed the slopes. Small ones, flung anywhere, lying around like kindling, The big trees, the ancient oaks, were fallen too, their roots flung upward to the sky. She had known it would happen. The wind had been so loud – the breath of it reaching even into the deep shaft – she could hardly believe it would not lift the whole lid off the hill and send it spinning out to sea like some crazy island.

"Hello?"

A voice – not the child's voice – calling to her. She stood up and looked around. Someone was waving at her; a person picking their way along the ramparts towards her, clambering round twisted thorn trees and ash branches. A woman, long hair catching the breeze. Anna waved to her.

"Hello!"

She stood watching as the woman came nearer. She was older than Anna, maybe in her 50s or 60s, wearing sturdy green trousers and a weatherbeaten green jacket. Her long hair was silver; it seemed odd to let it hang loose when the wind was blowing. Wisps kept flying into her eyes and she moved them away. When she was a few feet away from Anna, she stopped and smiled. Anna regarded her warily.

"Are you okay?" the woman asked. "Are you hurt? Anything broken – anything need bandaging?"

Her voice was crisp and assured: a Girl Guide voice. Anna, long beyond caring or knowing if anything was broken or needed bandaging, shook her head.

"Terrible thing," said the woman, nodding her head at the drowned valley. "How did you stay safe? Are your family – "

Anna shook her head again. "They went long ago," she said. She wasn't sure if she wanted to give her hiding place away to this woman. She might need it again. She might need it tonight. She had nowhere to sleep, right now, and in her rucksack were a banana and three energy bars.

"We have a bunker, on the farm," said the woman. "Well – an old air raid shelter. We took everything in and just hunkered down. It was the worst yet. By far the worst. The barn is gone. All the trees are down. I mean, we couldn't save all the animals – we couldn't – I mean we brought the dogs down with us, and that's it really. That's all."

Her crisp voice cracked a little, and she put a hand to her mouth. "I can't quite take in the scale of it. There isn't even anything we can do, right now. To rebuild, or clear away, or anything. But at least we're on dry land. I thought I'd walk up here and see how bad it is elsewhere. I never expected this."

They stood together, staring out at the clean expanse of water. Ripples ran across it, cats-paws pushed by the wind.

"It's very beautiful," said the woman, wonderingly.

"My house is under there," said Anna, pointing to the land strip.

"I'm so sorry," said the woman.

"It's nothing, really," said Anna, and realised that was true. "Nothing to what's already happened." Her legs began to tremble again.

"I have to sit down," she said. "Would you like a cigarette?"

The woman watched as she sat back down on the grass and began taking things out of the rucksack. Somewhere at the bottom was a packet of Marlborough Reds. She had smoked some of them last night, but not all. She fished it out at last, a little dented, and retrieved two cigarettes and her lighter.

"Well," said the woman. "I haven't smoked for 20 years."

"Me neither," said Anna. "Would you like one anyway?"

Carefully, the woman lowered herself down until she was sitting beside Anna and accepted the cigarette. She held it out for Anna to light. Now she was nearer, Anna could see that she was trembling all over. Her hand shivered and wavered as she held the cigarette, and it took Anna a few attempts to light it. When the tip was glowing, the woman took a long breath. She held it and blew it out with a sigh,

"My goodness," she said in her collected, RP voice. Princess Margeret, thought Anna, not Girl Guides. "That is rather lovely."

Anna nodded, lighting her own. They sat in silence, breathing in smoke and breathing it out. The tendrils of smoke curled away in the wind, spiralling away into nothing.

"We used to smoke to stay thin," said the woman. "Coffee, cigarettes and gin. What a diet! God we were thin. We used to racket through London in these little dresses, dancing over the pavements like angels. We thought we were goddesses. Look at me now. "

She stretched out her hand, staring at its persistent shiver and shake, the age-spots on her skin. Anna looked at her. Her long hair shone like frost in the sun, and she still had a strong jawline and a straight nose: the face of a woman who might indeed have been worshipped when she was young.

"We used to smoke because we weren't supposed to," Anna said. "Everyone knew by then it could kill you, and we - I don't know, maybe we wanted to die. We thought we were being rebellious."

The woman glanced at her. "My children never smoked," she said. "They never drank either. Great puritans. And look," she added, taking a last drag of the cigarette before stubbing it out firmly on a damp piece of turf and carefully putting the filter into her pocket, "what their reward has been. How many people do you think died last night? How many bodies are there, floating in there?"

They stared out at the water again. Drowned

villages. Anna remembered reading about a village in Wales that had been drowned, where the church-bells could still be heard at certain tides. Under that flat, sunlit expanse of water were the churches and their bells, the streets and the old cinema, the parks and their rusting play equipment.

When she looked closely, she could see the water broken here and there by the tops of buildings; blocks of flats. There hadn't been many of them left living so close to the sea. A few hundred? A thousand? How many of them had fled? Before she came up the hill she had gone to ask her 90 year old neighbour to come with her. Joyce had refused. "I was born here," she said from her easy chair, "and I'll die here if I must. I'm going to drink this bottle of gin, dear, and go to bed, and if I wake in the morning I wake. If not – so be it. Here – take that bottle of whisky. It was my husband's. I've never liked whisky and I've no need for it now. We could all do with a drink tonight."

So Anna had taken the whisky and her rucksack, and left her home as the sky turned yellow and the clouds piled up over the horizon, and the interminable alerts sounded from her phone.

"Do you think it would be different, "said Anna, "if women had been in charge?"

The woman snorted. "No. I don't think we're any better than men. We eat each other alive."

"I think things would be different," said Anna. "If we'd tried harder, maybe. If we'd fought more, to get things right."

"You can't fight a tidal wave," said the woman. "All you can do is run."

85

"I don't know," said Anna. "I don't want to - let go. Of everything. I don't want to run. I didn't run. I stayed, until they evacuated the school and the last children left. I was a teacher, you see. "

They sat quietly again. Anna closed her eyes, feeling the warmth of the sun on her cheek. Her mouth tasted of smoke and whisky. She needed to clean her teeth. Here she was, alive, after everything. After sickness, after catastrophe, after flood and storm and utter destruction. What had the little girl survived, down in the mineshaft? What had the kestrel meant to her? What angry gods had picked up her world like a ball and thrown it down, watching it split and shatter?

"Oh," said the woman softly and Anna opened her eyes again. "Look," said the woman. Anna looked. A few feet away, perched near the edge of the rampart, was a robin. It cocked its head and regarded them with a bright black eye.

"He survived the night too," said Anna. "Hidden in a hedge, maybe, close to the ground. "

She felt in her pocket and dug out a few crumbs of biscuit scattering them before the bird. It pecked up a couple, hopping closer to them. When it was within a few inches of Anna's foot it took flight, darting away down the hill into the ring of gorse-bushes surrounding the mineshaft.

"Where is your home, little bird?" asked Anna. "Home," she thought. *"Hold. Hold it fast, find it at home. The bird is flown."*

"Would you like to see something?" she asked the woman.

9
Tom Ackerman

Kevin stared through the window behind his computer, watching one pigeon bow to another. The office clattered and whirred about him, yet he was a twig on its tumultuous currents. He was here, yet only by habit.

In terms of productivity he was done. Not with work, he'd barely made a dent in the twenty four emails he'd walked into this morning.

"He must be emotionally drained," his had colleagues muttered. "He's come back too soon. He needs more time."

Not that he blame them for thinking that, but he can't keep doing nothing.

His workmates talked as they typed. Gossip and banter flowed like new wine. But to him, their good humours tasted only of vinegar. Even the pigeons seemed obnoxiously jovial. And now was just not the time for that.

Kevin dragged his mind from the pigeons and attempted another email.

Hi Kevin,
I know you're really busy, but Stephen asked me to let you know he wants the report on Custom Motors

by 16:00. Also can you blah, blah. Blah, blah.

The words huddled together on the screen, blurring at the edges, conspiring against him in the haze of his mind. His stomach growled in indignation.

Sod it. Stephen could wait.

He rose, plucking the Tupperware from his bag, and ambled across the office to the microwave. As the previous night's dinner warmed, Kevin fell into the middle distance, letting his thoughts drift. This would be the fourth lunch of left-overs in as many days. He sniffed. Cooking was not a past-time he particularly enjoyed, that had been left that to Robin. The microwave interrupted his nostalgia.

The scent of Chinese greeted him, but his mind did not return the warm welcome. The world was bland and monochrome. Old delights were empty. His commute to work, once vibrant and bright, now a patchwork of dark, dull shades of who-cares-grey. When and how he pulled the little box of food from the microwave he wasn't sure.

The walk back to his cubicle was not long, but his colleagues watched him warily. The slight turn of the head at the pass of his reflection, the not-so-subtle glance over the top of a partition, the tight pulling of lips and the pathetic looks of sympathy. All unwelcome reminders that they knew.

He sank down into his chair, and pulled a fork from the pen-pot beside him. He took stony mouthful after stony mouthful, the flavours falling from the noodles like old leaves. Monochrome once again.

"That smells good," Paul commented. His work neighbour for the past few years, Paul had crossed the space between the desks surfing the wheels of his chair.

"Just Chow-mein," Kevin responded.

"Well," Paul said, his tone light and breezy, "beats a peanut butter sandwich, don't it?" He gestured to his small lunchbox. Kevin grunted.

"How you doing today?" Paul questioned. Had he known the complexity of the question he had just asked, Kevin wondered if Paul would have uttered it in the first place.

"Fine," Kevin said.

"I was surprised to see you in today. Thought you'd not be back for a few weeks yet."

Kevin spiked another forkful of Chow-mein, but said nothing,

"So..." Paul said. "Look I just wanted to say: I'm sorry."

Kevin chewed.

"I just thought," Paul started, grasping for words, "if people knew then they'd give you some space. Give you time. I just wanted to try and do what was best"

"Well you didn't."

The edge on Kevin's words hadn't been intended but he didn't apologise for it either.

"I know mate, and I'm sorry," Paul said. "I just wanted you to know." There was a soft rumble as Paul rolled back to his desk.

Kevin continued eating, slow deliberate scoops of flavour-blind food. Chewed, swallowed, but not enjoyed. He had hoped to come back unnoticed. He had hoped to carry on, to find some sense of normality in this maddening refuge. But that chance had been unintentionally robbed from him, and now they all knew.

Beside him, pinned to the blue velvet partition, a grey cat sunned itself in a puddle of light on a kitchen floor. On its right, a red-headed woman giggled as his former self blew raspberries into her neck. Gaze hooked by the shock of scarlet, he barely registered the rogue noodle slithering between the fork spines, dropping limply onto his tie.

"Did you read my email?" Stephan asked, the words spilling from his lips like tar from a barrel. Kevin's line manager had, it seemed, tried to approach the desk with as little warning of his presence as possible. That Kevin had not been startled by his sudden question seemed only to annoy the man more. He barely looked up.

"The Custom Motors re–"

"Report, yes," Stephen cut in. "Where is it?"

"I've just got to finish–"

"Why don't I have it?"

"I've been..." Kevin started, but the words died on his lips.

"Well?" The middle-manager paused, but to no avail. He pulled sharply on the lapel of his suit jacket, pushing his chin out like a self-absorbed rooster.

"If I have to remind you, you're already late," he stated with self-importance.

"Sorry," Kevin muttered.

"Besides," Stephen eyed the chow-mein, sneering, "can't be buying take out if we're unemployed now, can we?" He laughed at his joke and sauntered off.

"Prick," Kevin muttered. He finished his lunch in silence, until his bladder compelled him to move.

It took a few seconds for him to clock the note on his return. He was sat back in his creaky desk chair, just reaching for his mouse, when he noticed it. Garish yellow against the dark charcoal of the computer, the post-it was a beacon of abnormality.

The bird has flown,
In search of true pleasure,
How vainly he'll roam.
To hold it for life,
He must find it at home.

Kevin stared at it for a long minute before he plucked it from the screen. For a moment, he considered crumpling the note, but it stuck to him.

Where had it come from was the obvious question. Who'd written it the next. He'd only been gone a minute, and when he'd returned the office had seemed in a similar state to when he'd left. So who'd written the note? He had seen that writing before, and recently, but the memory was obscured. He leant back, holding the note delicately. The handwriting looked feminine. Too loopy for the men either side of him. It definitely wasn't Paul's. But, he knew seen it before. Of that he was certain.

He glanced up at the picture beside him. Robin would know. She'd always had a knack for puzzles. Unable to leave her bed, she'd poured over them for hours as he worked, placing piece after piece, a look of mad satisfaction playing on her face. He'd fallen into the habit of bringing her the puzzle page of *The Metro* on his way home from work.

They would sit in bed together, poring over Jigsaws and Crosswords and Sudoku. She would cling to them like a terrier until, after much tugging and poking, she'd wriggled the solution from its hiding place. He treasured those looks of triumph. In those moments they would be happy, and he could pretend that it would last for ever.

He turned the note over between his fingers, eyeing the second and third line.

In search of true pleasure,
How vainly he'll roam.

They'd got the cat shortly after Robin's third sick note. With Robin's health slowly declining, he'd thought a pet would bring back some joy when he was at work. And, for a time, the mass of fur and purrs had done so. He was a scrawny little thing. The fur around one eye was thin, his spine clearly felt below the mass of long graphite fur. They'd watched as he'd sniffed about their tiny flat, poking his nose into every dusty corner and dark crevice he could find. Exhausted, he'd clambered onto Robin's lap and dozed, purring loudly as her gentle fingers combed his coat. Jeeves. Robin had suggested the name on a whim, spotting a patch of black fur just below the creature's neck.

"It looks like a bow tie," Robin had argued.

"And that makes him a butler?"

"Yes."

And so it had been decided, and Jeeves had been named. Kevin had come home on many an occasion to see Robin and Jeeves curled in bed together fast asleep. Again there was a fleeting hope that this would be it. They could stay like this always. They had tried for that. Fought for that. But in the end life had gotten the better of them.

"Kevin?" The female voice jolted him from his thoughts.

"Hmm?" he looked up. Jen blinked at him, concern floating behind kind eyes.

"I said: would you like tea or coffee?"

"Oh, right. Sorry." He looked for his mug. "Erm, coffee, please." Taking the mug, she went to leave, but stopped, turned back, and placed a hand on his shoulder.

"For what it's worth," she said, swallowing hard. "I am truly sorry." She squeezed his shoulder, turned, and walked away.

The comment struck him like a slap to the face. He'd so desperately hoped to avoid this, the condolences and special treatment.

I'm not the one who's... who's...

But the thought got caught on his breath, snagging at it, making it leap.

They'd thought things were getting better. She was there to see his little brother married. They'd rented a small *B&B* close to the venue and had sat, late into the evening, watching swallows play in the twilight. She had rested her head on his shoulder and they'd had hope.

"You know," she had said. "We should think about getting married."

"Mhum," he'd responded. Then after a pause, "did you just ask me to marry you?"

She giggled, "I think I just did." She angled her face up to look at him, dark eyes searching his reaction. "And?"

"Sure, why not?" he'd said. "But you're getting me a ring."

They'd laughed and, for a moment, they'd dared to believe things would work out. That things would be okay. But that was a fantasy, and real life could be cruel.

Kevin closed his eyes and struggled to regain his emotions. They were stallions, or wraiths, and if not controlled, they would overrun him. Besides, this was neither the time nor the place for that.

He focused on the note. Where had he seen this before? Heard this before? It nagged, pulled, fought for air in the cold currents of his unsettled mind. But it was lost.

Jen returned, inky coffee in the mug. He smiled his thanks, turning back to stare at the note.

To hold it for life,
He must find it at home.

It was true he'd been spending more time at work lately. The house was too painful. Too raw. Too empty. He'd barely slept in the last few weeks. He'd roll over and reach out for Robin only to panic when she wasn't there. Jeeves had started to sleep on her pillow. Maybe he missed her presence? Maybe, like Kevin, he just wanted to be close to the one thing that still retained her scent. It was difficult to tell.

Despite himself, Kevin smiled. Robin would have laughed to see him jump as the cat's tail tickled his nose in the small hours of the morning. He could barely remember the sound of her laughter. Her smile he could picture clear as ice, but it had been too long since he'd heard her laugh.

When she'd deteriorated, she'd done so with the speed and grace of a freefall sky-diver. The pain had racked her body both day and night, stabbing through the soft tissue of her side, causing her to cry out. It had sapped the strength from her muscle fibres. Drained her of her reserves. Then it had gone for her organs.

It was an organised coup of her body. Her heart rate would spike, her lungs would stop and he would be forced to pray for her breath to return. He'd been powerless to stop it.

"It will be alright," she'd told him. "I'm used to them these days."

But in the end he'd called for an ambulance, despite her protests.

"Don't let them take me Kev," She'd begged him. "Don't let them take me from here. From you."

"It's okay, Robin" he'd reassured her, holding her hand, repeating that same lie over and over again. "It'll be okay."

He knew it wouldn't. He'd known, as they sped off for the hospital, that there would be no recovery. Known that the only person waiting for them would be holding a scythe. But he'd refused to give in. To give up hope.

She died in the ambulance.

He'd clutched her hand so tightly, he'd not noticed her grip slip away until the cabin was ringing with alarms. He'd been pushed aside as the paramedics did their best, but in the end she'd gone. She'd been set free. Released from this mortal coil, never to hold his hand again, or be in pain, or run her fingers through his hair. The rest of that night passed him in blur. He'd sat outside the entrance to A & E, as stretchers and trollies trundled past, their occupants still clinging to the hope of salvation. But his had gone.

"You got that report yet Kevin?" Stephen demanded. The sudden utterance behind his head brought Kevin back to the present with a jolt.

"Sorry?" He asked. A flash of satisfaction twitched at the corner of the managers lips.

"I said," he repeated, "where is my report?"

Kevin's mouth opened to speak, but the words were trapped behind the lump in his throat.

"Whatever have you been doing all day?" Stephan

asked, a slug-like eyebrow climbing his forehead.

Again words failed Kevin and he simply gestured to the computer. Stephen rolled his eyes and twisted fat lips into a smirk.

"Kevin if you're not going to do any work, why are you even here?"

The words of the note flashed through Kevin's mind.

Find it at home.

"I," he said slowly. "I don't know." Kevin stood up, his sudden movement taking the manager by surprise.

"What do you think you're doing?" Stephen asked, aghast.

Kevin shrugged.

"Going home."

Stephen blustered and flapped, shouting angry protests and garbled warnings, but Kevin had gone.

Rain had fallen constantly since 7am that morning. Now, however, the sun had burnt away the worst of the clouds and the air smelt crisp and earthy. As Kevin walked, the colour returned to his world. Emeralds shone in rough chocolate trees, birds sang ballads to one another, and the wind whispered sweet nothings around his ears.

Tonight he would go home to his cat. A cat who loved him, who did not understand why two humans had become one, and why one was never home. He would go home, pull out old photographs and remember.

He would not hide from this, as it refused to hide from him. His grief and guilt had followed him like hounds for weeks, but no more. Why? Why hide from something that will not stop hunting you?

His train ride home was flecked with mixed emotions. He scrolled through old photos and let the wild horses of his mind run wild. In a commute he visited their first date; their first movie night; the time he'd fallen in the canal showing off; the time she'd got ice-cream on her nose and hadn't realised; the time they were woken by a pony at 5am and then giggled for hours. He saw her smile, and scream, and laugh, and pout. He visited her tears after a showing of *Marley and Me* and felt his own, both happy and sad, mix on the canvas of his cheek.

On his arrival home, Jeeves greeted him with a loud chirrup and a series of hungry meows, curling himself around his ankles.

"Alright boy," Kevin cooed. "I know, I know. Food time, come on."

The cat bounded ahead, fluffy body leaping up onto the back of the sofa, running expertly across the countertop to perch by the cupboard door. Kevin opened the door and Jeeves nuzzled his elbow. Filling the bowl, Kevin placed it down and stepped out of the way as the cat leapt down.

Something crunched underfoot.

The shattered body of a picture frame lay broken on the floor, shards of glass and plastic spread out over the vinyl. Kevin sighed.

"And I suppose you're going to tell me this wasn't you, eh?"

Jeeves made no effort to reply, fully focused on the snippets of meat and jelly in his bowl.

Kevin picked up the broken picture frame, assessing the damage. The frame was finished but the picture was still intact. He smiled, remembering their first Christmas with Jeeves. Robin had insisted on taking a family photo. She'd even ordered a little Christmas cat jumper, which Jeeves looked less than impressed wearing. They'd been happy. Hopeful, even then. Kevin plucked the picture from the frame, discarding the broken casing in the bin and laying he picture on the countertop.

Collecting a dustpan from beneath the sink, Kevin set to clearing up the glass, the tiny shards singing their indignation at their removal. In a blur of movement Jeeves leapt upon the counter top and bolted for his windowsill, knocking the picture as he dashed past.

Kevin watched as the picture tumbled, twirling in mid-air, landing face down on the pile of glass.

"Cheers, bud," he muttered to the cat, now sat on the windowsill grooming his tail. Kevin rolled his eyes and reached for the picture once again.

He froze.

There, on the back of the photo, in her neat printed letters, Robin had printed a caption:

Jeeve's First Christmas

And below, in smaller letters:

In search of true pleasure,

How vainly he'll roam.
To hold it for life,
He must find it at home.

10
Petula Mitchell

The bus to Worthing rattled along the main road as rain sheeted down. The wind was relentless, and trees still full of their summer crown of leaves bent and swayed under their own sodden weight. Chloe was the only one on the top deck and was considering beating a retreat to the lower deck. Her bravado about sitting at the front of the double decker had all but dissolved as the low hanging branches dashed against the windscreen. The whole vehicle felt unstable to her, but that was probably due to an over active imagination. She could see herself clinging on for dear life to the bars in front of her as the bus toppled sideways with a grinding of metal and crash of splintering glass. She shook her head, and scolded herself for being ridiculous.

As she made her descent of the narrow winding stairs, her shoes clanking on the metal treads, she bumped into a man coming up. He walked straight into her and showed no inclination to reverse down and let her pass. There was a moment of stand off as they stood and stared at each other. Not that she could see much of his face. Dark glasses covered him from the brows to below the cheekbones and a wide brimmed hat sat on top of the frames. She could just see a thin lipped mouth that looked unaccustomed to smiling. Chloe sighed and backed up the four steps onto the top deck to let the stranger pass. As she did so he doffed his hat and managed to curl a humourless smile out of his pallid features. Chloe's stop was coming up fast now. She didn't return the smile or say a word. She completed her journey to the lower deck, ringing the bell as she went and stepped off into the wet afternoon. The light was failing early and as the bus pulled away she looked up to see if she could catch sight of the stranger. There was no sign of anybody on the top deck at all.

Once indoors Chloe started to remove her soaked coat and looked for a towel to dry her handbag. She noticed the zip was half open on the bag. She was very fastidious about fastening it and kept the bag close to her for fear of pick pockets. A folded sheet of blue paper stuck out of the top. It looked like the Basildon Bond writing paper her mother used to use. The edge of it was damp and a darker shade than the rest. She had no idea how it got there.

In search of true pleasure
How vainly we roam.
To hold it for life,
we must find it at home.
The bird has flown.

She read the note twice and the second reading of it did not make her any less puzzled. She presumed it must have been put there by the man on the bus, as it was the only interaction she had been involved in during her journey. But to what end she could not imagine. She contemplated ripping it up and putting it in the kitchen bin, then thought no. She didn't know why but suddenly the message felt important. The bird has flown. What bird? Where has it gone? Why was it given to her?

The following day found Chloe making her way to the library. The weather had made a complete volte face and it was sparkling autumn sunshine that met her at the door. The piece of paper was safely folded and tucked inside her bag. She switched off the radio, which was playing 'Summer Nights' from Grease. It was the latest hit from the film and frankly, she thought, a lot of nonsense. Chloe preferred punk bands, enjoying the music, but not liking the clothes. It was Saturday and the library would probably be busy. One of her friends was an archivist there and might be able to throw some light on the strange message she had taken possession of. The encounter with the peculiar man on the bus had left Chloe slightly unnerved but nevertheless intrigued.

As Chloe entered the library she could see her friend Alison behind the counter. The doors had only been open for five minutes and just a couple of people were settling down to read the newspapers left out for public perusal. Their conversation had to be kept low to avoid the glares of the early readers.

"Alison, how are you?" Chloe began.

"I'm fine. Intrigued by what you told me on the phone last night. Have you got the ditty?"

Chloe reached into her bag and handed over the now dry piece of paper.

"Does it mean anything to you?" she asked.

"Strangely it does! You know where I live?"

"Yes. In Warwick Gardens. Of course I know." Chloe said.

"Well this is engraved on a stone a few yards from my house. It's from an eighteenth century poem by Edward Moore about the joys of being married to an obedient wife. Apparently it was very popular and was turned into a song. The bird has flown bit though...that is an add on. I don't know about that."

" Why would a complete stranger give this to me?" Chloe asked her friend.

"Hey, I might be a mine of useless information but I'm not psychic. Your mysterious man and all that is something you will have to solve. Go and have a look at the inscription. You might get some inspiration."

"From a block of stone? I have my doubts. I should probably just throw this in the bin and forget it."

"I get a feeling you aren't going to though." said Alison.

Chloe shrugged and turned to go. At that moment through the glass doors she caught sight of the mysterious man from the previous day. He still had the large hat and dark glasses on but he was looking straight at her with the same thin smile on his lips. She blinked, looked round at Alison and when she looked back he had gone. When she reached the outside she looked up and down the street and there was no sign of him. Now she was beginning to wonder if it had been a figment of her imagination. The paper though, that was real and tangible. Spurred on by renewed curiosity she made her way through the town to Warwick

Gardens and sought out the engraving that Alison had told her about. Sure enough, there were the very same words in stone. Chloe reached down to push back the weeds encroaching over the edge of the slab. There didn't seem to be anything special about the location in a quiet old residential street. If anything this morning had left her even more puzzled. She stood and looked around her willing a clue to come, but nothing did. As she left the road an old lady came out of her house.

"Another one!" she exclaimed.

"Excuse me?" replied Chloe.

"Another one looking at that old slab. You must be about the tenth one this week, just standing there looking at it all puzzled like. It's nothing special you know. It's just an old bit of nonsense put there years ago before any of us moved here. I've been here twenty years and there isn't nothing magical about it. I think the council should come and rip it up. If it's going to attract all sorts weirdos I don't want it near my house any more. It all started with a creepy looking character in a big hat, wearing sunglasses at night might I add. If that isn't suspicious I don't know what is. I said to my Albert, he's a wrong 'un. If ever there was a wrong 'un it was him. Of course Albert was no help, sat in front of the telly and not caring to move. By the time he got to the front parlour window the man was gone. I swear I could be kidnapped and it would be Christmas before that husband even noticed."

Before the woman could continue with her character assassination of her husband Chloe put her hand up and walked away. Her mind was now working overtime. How many people had been drawn to the spot by the stranger? More to the point, why?

"The bird has flown." she muttered to herself.

She decided that a walk along the sea front and onto the pier would clear her head. There was a faded Victorian charm about the place and if the tide was high the waves crashing on the shingle beach were a therapeutic noise.

The pier was a magical place to Chloe. The not quite land, not quite water feeling that she got as she strode towards the end of it and peered between the cracks in the wooden deck. She could hear the restless tide beneath her feet as water slapped and sloshed and whispered below her. The wind was lively and wrestled with her hair. As she turned the corner at the end of the pier to make a return journey back to the promenade, there he was. The stranger, his wide brimmed hat untroubled by the stiff breeze and the sun illuminating his pale mouth and jaw. She now realised how tall his black clad figure was as he loomed over her. She felt a jolt of fear, quickly followed by some anger at being led on a wild goose chase by this person. Or maybe she was angry at herself for getting drawn in by insatiable curiosity. Maybe her own life had become so dull and mundane she had turned it into an adventure of sorts to add some spice to her existence.

She held up the paper he had given her the previous day.

"Why me? What is this for and who are you anyway?" she asked.

There was no preamble to her questions. No social

niceties. He didn't seem perturbed at this though. Maybe he was used to people forgetting their manners around him. Chloe thought if you went around giving cryptic messages to people then you must be forever dealing with the fallout.

"The bird has flown....." he said.

"Yes I know the bloody bird has flown! But what does it mean? What do you want from me?"

"I want the bird to return, but I need help to find it." he replied.

"What makes you think I can make it return? Or find it? I know nothing about birds! This is ridiculous. I'm giving up my Saturday, scratching my head to solve a cryptic clue I got from somebody I don't know and have frankly had enough. I'm out of here. I'm going to find somewhere for coffee and a bun and forget I ever saw you or your stupid bit of paper!"

Chloe strode forward and was going to push past the stranger and return to the town. He blocked her way and for the first time showed what could be called some humanity.

"No, please don't. I need you to help. None of the others have been able to find her."

"What others?" Chloe shouted at him.

Her frustration was beginning to boil over. Part of her wanted to go and forget the whole thing, but that tugging feeling of curiosity just would not let go.

" The message. I have dropped it all over the town in different ways and in different times. All the people have been drawn to the stone. Each of them has got that far and given up. I search for my wife. My Lallha Rukh. My Tulip Cheeked beauty. I don't know what became of her. I have searched for two centuries to find her. My little bird has flown and I don't know where she has gone. Do you know what love is young lady? Its power to drive you on? It has, in the words of our favourite song , made me roam vainly to find her. I travel through space and time searching. I think that you could be the one to help me."

Chloe was now even more confused.

"I think you might need help, but not from me. You can't be that old. I think you are either just winding me up for some obscure reason or you are a very sick man. Now I'm going to give you the benefit of the doubt and say it's the later and just walk away. I hope you find whatever it is you are looking for, but I'm out of here."

She made to go, to stride off back along the pier and forget all this weirdness. However she found herself back in the town, back in the street where the stone slab was laid. In front of her a man in a loose cotton shirt and britches, his hair tied back , was standing over a piece of stone. He held a hammer and chisel and she heard him call out.

"Come see my love! I have finished it.!"

A woman appeared from the door of the house and went to his side to admire the work.

"Oh tis fine work William. Our favourite song cast forever in stone. Just as we heard it in Vauxhall pleasure gardens. Thomas Lowe had such a fine voice did he not?" she said.

"Indeed he did my sweet. Such a happy evening. We were so lucky to have had a fine honeymoon in London and to have found such contentment since. I swear I shall love you forever my Tulip, forever."

108

The woman glowed in his words and smiled at him. She went back indoors and he left the hammer and chisel in the garden and followed her. She wanted to follow them into the house but her feet would not move. She was aware of the dark figure behind her.

"You see how lovely she is? I miss her so much."

The next thing Chloe knew she was inside the house, but it was dark apart from two or three flickering candles. It was cold and she could hear rain lashing the window pane next to her. Raised voices came down the stairs.

"How could you do that? You would turn me into a cuckold! How could you let a man in to the house while I am away at business?"

"I did not William! Ask the man, ask the neighbours. I spoke to him upon the threshold and told him to return once you were home. I would not let a stranger into the house when you are away." the woman replied sounding desperate.

"You lie! You lie!" he yelled.

There was a sickening noise of metal striking metal and the woman let out a sound so awful Chloe thought she would remember it to her grave. On entering the room she found William standing over the body of the woman, the sharp chisel protruding from her head as he held the hammer. The dark figure was beside her.

"Great God! What did I do?" he asked.

"Your bird didn't fly. You never gave her the chance." Chloe answered flatly.

Suddenly she was on the pier again in the breezy autumn sunshine. The dark figure was gone and she still clutched the piece of paper. She looked at it, but it was now blank. She looked around and she was quite alone. Everything seemed quite normal. She headed back towards the town putting the blue paper in a bin as she went. As she passed the arcade she could hear the music they were playing. You're the one that I want.... blared from the speakers.

11

Cariad Parsonage

Genre: Crime fiction
Characters: Narrator, Thursday, Avery and I'd-rather-not-say-actually.

Part 1

One cold winter's morning our detective is taking a chilly stroll through Worthing, the wind rapidly becoming closer to blowing her hat off, she takes determined strides through the whirling gales.

Earlier this morning the detective, whose name we do so find out is Thursday, is doing the mundane but ,in this case, important task of washing the dishes...

It had become a problem. If she put it off any more she feared she may not be able to open her door (ooh that rhymed). Forcing herself to think it wouldn't take too long, it can't be too hard and anyway they're just dishes, she plunged her hands into the abyss and 2 hours later she pulled them out as wrinkly as a raisin.

Let's take a side note here reader and talk about Thursday. Like everyone, surely, Thursday notes down everything ever she has ever done as is doing now in a growing collection of tiny little notebooks. This had been a habit ever since she realised that people forget things, and being very headstrong she decided she wanted no more of that nonsense and put a stop to it.

So being Thursday, Thursday was stopping every 30 seconds to pick up a dripping wet pen in her soapy hands and scribble wildly on the open page. At this very moment Thursday was writing that she could hear lovely birdsong outside the window and- wait a minute it's winter! Thursday scrabbled for a towel and fumbled her phone out of her pocket, Hello? Silence. Excuse me if this is a jo-

'The bird-' a deep voice boomed down the speaker.

'Just spam mail,' sighed Thursday, 'honestly people sometimes'.

Part 2

The wind flung her notebook out of her hand and landed open on the page about birds (our Thursday was thoroughly interested in them and had always wanted to do bird watching). When it was flung out of her hand Thursday had been writing about the mysterious phone call and the bird song (do not forget readers that our Thursday is a detective and to her this was like something out of a case).

Oi, narrator get out of my bit! Shoo! Also how do you know so much?

Did you not get my warning! Dear readers do not listen to her! She does not know what she's got herself into............ Phew, he's gone, now back to my story...

So as you can imagine when I walked past a rather cool (it thought) picture of a bird spray- painted on the side of the bank, I just had to photograph it.

'The bird has flown' it read in those hard to reader spray-painter letters.

Part 3

'I, Thursday, declare my allegiance to the local birdwatching committee, to be its loyal leader, protector and founder   for many years,' declared Thursday and a round of 2 people clapping echoed in the dismal local hire-a-hall.

'So,' said Avery, 'now you are a proper member of the local bird watching committee, which by the way is a boring name we'll have to change it, let's organise our next meeting and we really need to look at getting more members by the way.'

'Hmm.. on the subject of naming it,' speculated Thursday and showed her the picture from earlier. 'That's so cool!!!' screamed the 3rd member of the group, far to excited for 07:00 at night. 'Oh, yes,' started Avery 'this is, this, is...what's your name again?'

'Oh, I'm, I'm...I'd rather not say actually,' said I'd-rather-not-say-actually.

'I think we are at a collective decision to call our group, The birds have flown!' announced Avery.

 Local news at your doorstep whenever you need it!
A new bird watching committee down in Worthing!
Meetings between 06:00 and 07:00 on a
Thursday!
Join, 'The bird has flown' !

113

12

Joe Bunn

"We should move that next." Edward was pointing to the large walnut unit on the back wall.

"We should empty it first." I replied, as I walked over to where he was standing. He knocked on the top and let the hollow sound ring.

"Seems pretty empty to me."

I tutted, and rolled my eyes as if I were a cartoon. There was clearly something in the thing. I could smell it as I opened the doors. It smelt like soft biscuits and reminded me of orange squash and peony wallpaper.

We had been clearing out my mum's old house for about three days now. We were doing it in order, and so far it had been incredibly boring. First day, we cleared all the actual rubbish out. Old magazines that weren't old enough to be valuable, crisp packets that would induce nostalgia,

Dried flannels and mummified apple cores. Second day was all about sorting the paperwork. Letters from old lovers to one side, Then it was devices. So off went the phones and leads and leads for phones. And we were onto furniture. The big job, that, for the most part, Ed had been skiving out of.

He was meant to be the muscle. That was the plan anyway, I'd be the one pointing towards stuff, like a table or an anvil, say, and he'd lift it up and put it outside. He was the muscle, by merit of the fact his arms were ever so slightly bigger than mine. No such luck here, however. So far, he had identified a couple of futons that had been placed on their sides, and pointed out a couple of things with his feet. Not much lifting going on, though. I was still looking in the cupboard. It contained the classics.

"Old tin." I passed it out. "Videos." I passed these out one at a time, reading the labels as I went. *"Toy Story. Gone with the Wind. The Hand that rocks the Cradle."* I hesitated before handing over the last one. "The bird has flown. I've never heard of that one. And it says 'do not erase' here."

"Yeah. I've not heard of that either. I don't reckon it's a film." Ed was turning over the video in his hands like it would turn an invisible mechanism inside the plastic and open up, revealing the secrets within. He stopped to look at the label again. "And there's this picture of a bird.

"And you know what...?" Ed just walked off, not waiting for my surely brilliant first guess at the answer to his question.

"Right." I carried on pulling the other clutter from the unit, sorting into little piles as I went. Useless piles. The sort that make you feel like you're doing something when you're not. I could hear Ed outside now, he was in the skip. It had that true skip-dipping sound of paper rustling, with a side of unfathomable clunking. I tried out my second cartoon movement of the day, putting my hand on my hip and shaking my head, which was hard to do whilst kneeling. I carried on sorting cupboard items. I had a good set of piles now, descending in size.

"Here it is! I knew I'd seen one somewhere!"

"What?" I didn't look up.

"This!" said Ed. I turned to face him, he was waving something silver and rectangular. "A video player. For the video."

"Ah right, cool."

"I'll get this set up, you can make us a tea."

Ed hadn't used his slightly-bigger-than-mine muscles to move the big flowery sofa yet so I sank into its charms whilst Ed put on the video. It had that satisfying clomp as it inhaled the tape. Ed sank into the seat next to me as the familiar white static bars faded from the screen and our show started.

It is a clearly homemade film, we know because the person filming walks from in front to behind the camera. They are wearing a black and white striped shirt. It is in black and white. The shot shows a bed. It is only slightly larger than a double. The person behind the camera speaks.

'In search of true pleasure, how vainly we roam, to hold it for life, we must find it at home.' There is an accent. Northern maybe? American?

Then a woman walks in front of the camera. She is barely stifling a laugh. She is also naked.

She lays on the bed, still naked. You can't really

make out her face, her long dark hair is in the way.
The striped top is thrown, crumpled up, from behind
the camera. It lands on the woman. She sweeps her
hair out of her eyes.

"Where do I know her from?" said Ed. "I swear I know her from something."

"Me too." I extricated myself from the gullet of the sofa and leant in closer to the screen, to look at this woman's face. "It better not be porn you're thinking of." I turned back round to Ed with a pantomime glare. His face went white.

"Oh, oh no." He pointed at the screen.

"Don't be silly, I don't really care."

"No. I know who it is."

"Who?"

"Your mum."

"Don't joke."

"No, Julia, it's your mum."

I turned back to the TV just in time to catch a man's naked bum flounce across the screen as my young mum's giggling face became instantly recognisable to me. In one swift motion I kicked the television square on the manbum, causing it to short and switch off.

"At least you turned it off before the stuff happened."

"What?"

"You know, the big stuff."

"My mum wasn't the stuff sort."

117

"She looked a right sort in that video."

"Can we not talk about this any more?"

"Sure."

"Can we continue moving the things please?"

"Sure."

"Are you still thinking about my mum's boobs?"

"Never."

"Are you?"

"A bit. They looked a bit like yours. Only worse. All old fashioned and pointy."

"No more boob talk."

"Okay."

Two days. It was two days before the intrigue got the better of me. We didn't go back to the house in those two days. It was like I'd seen a ghost there, not just some back-from-the-grave bedroom frolics. Two days, and I had to know. Oh, plus one more day of arguing with myself about whether rewatching a homemade porno featuring my mum made me a pervert, a maniac or a bit of both. But there were too many unanswered questions not to. And hey, maybe it wasn't porn, there was that arty part at the start after all. So after two days, and a day of deliberation, I had to know who that man was, and I had the perfect way to find out without becoming a perverted maniac. I'd make Ed do it.

I decided that returning to where we left off would be a bad idea, so I retrieved the video, and player from mum's and brought it back to ours. I sat Ed down on our less mouth-like sofa, made sure he was sat up straight, and put myself in a chair facing away from the TV at more than leg distance away from the screen. I didn't rewind, I just pressed play from where we'd left off. I also called Ed down to watch it maybe 30 seconds before it started, so he had no time to realise what was going on.

"If this is some sick idea of foreplay, it's not going to work on me."

"Give over. That's not why we're doing this. Just keep watching."

"Well, maybe it'll work a bit."

"Shut up and watch."

"Okay."

"And describe it to me."

"Okay."

I watched the TV's light flickering in Ed's eyes like a rubbish strobe, and tried to figure out what the shapes could be. He was concentrating hard, frowning slightly. And now a bit more.

"So the bloke's come in. He's naked. Can't see his penis beneath that bush. And the long hair too. He's wearing little round glasses and... hold on."

"What's up?" I asked, touching his knee.

"It's weird, but I think I know who it is." He bowed himself forward, to see better. "Yeah, it's definitely him."

He looked so pleased with himself, a smug half grin like a baby does. He hadn't told me.

"Who?"

"It's John Lennon."

"What?"

"John Lennon."

"What?"

I span around in my chair so fast I knocked the video player off the side. It threw up the video like it was a black pellet of vomit in a video, which hit the floor and splashed out into a thousand pixels. Ed took the opportunity,

"That's what I call *Norwegian Wood.*"

Me and Ed were stood over the parts of the video player with the smashed up black plastic bits of the video laid out on the kitchen counter. It was an anatomical diagram in 3D. I nudged a bit of the tape from the inside with a finger.

"And you're sure that it was John Lennon?" I put my finger inside the tape reel and examined it as if I was an expert in video repair. Ed had a look of barely disguised excitement on his face.

"I'm sure of it. 1000%."He knew I hated it when he used anything over 100%. I resisted the urge to correct him.

"How?"

"He had the glasses. The nose. The voice."

"John Lennon? Out of the Beatles?"

"No, John Lennon out of the Plastic Ono band. That's why it started off like some performance art piece, right?" Ed said, showing a knowledge of Beatles lore I didn't know he had. "Yes, THE John Lennon."

I paced away from the table, if taking one step away

120

from the table and then back can be called pacing. I considered other people it could have been, but only came up with one possibility: his son, Julian Lennon. Maybe my dad? But then, Could it have been Ringo Starr?

I snorted derisively, the third cartoon thing I'd do that week.

Ed got up and put his hands on my arms, pinning them gently to my sides and caught my worried gaze.

"Look," he said, trying to keep eye contact, "the fact of the matter is your mum had some fun before you were born, as all mums do, yours just happened to have a higher class of fun." A thought occurred to me.

"Did they even have home video cameras back then?"

"What?"

"I mean, they didn't have the cameras to make this video. Certainly not a VHS camera."

"I don't think you want to think about that."

"Why?"

"They had cameras back then, especially someone like Lennon would have. But they would have been on reels. That means your mum got this film transferred to video."

"Gross."

"Weird she hadn't made the leap to DVD yet. But there we go."

"Can we stop talking about this now?"

"Sure."

Ed opened the foil and film drawer, and pulled a roll of

121

large sandwich bags from beneath the parchment paper. He ripped off a bag, shook it open, then used his arms to scoop the bits of black plastic and tape into it. He squeezed the air out as best he could, then tied the top. He opened the junk drawer at the other end of the kitchen, pulled a marker out and went to write on the label. It didn't work, so he put it back into the drawer. I resisted the urge to tell him not to. He pulled another marker out, and wrote 'MUM LENNON PORN' on it. He then put both of the items into the drawer. He did all of this without saying anything, then turned to me.

"That's got to be worth money right?"

He closed the drawer.

And that was all I could think about for the next week. We went back to my mum's then, we were rapidly running out of time and we'd not been there for a while. Why? Was I scared of finding another film? Perhaps a video of her robbing a bank with Bruce Springsteen? Getting drunk with Cilla Black? And why would I be frightened to find those? They'd be worth money without the weird incest bit. I'm ashamed to say, I hardly thought about my real live actual mum in the situation. Maybe it was because she'd be laughing in the bit I saw her in, seemed happy. She had always been quite a introverted person, especially towards the end, but in that video she had been laughing. A real laugh as well, so I didn't feel the need to worry about her. I just worried about the money.

We moved more furniture. We left the walnut unit until last. Slowly painting ourselves until there was that, and one chair, with a stuffed pigeon on it. Cyril, the taxidermied pigeon had always freaked me out as a child, but nothing could freak me as much as my mum in bed with a Beatle. Seemingly, we'd been blind to that chair before now.

"We'll need to move that next." said Edward, pointing to the chair. Stating the obvious, really. Of course, he didn't do much to help me achieve this, not by moving what was on it. So I sighed loudly, in my bi weekly cartoon movement, and picked up Cyril and plonked him in the black bin bag I was holding. Hello, goodbye Cyril.

Then I looked back at the chair. It was unusual. The seat had features.

It was a chair in the shape of a face. A face I recognised, clearly.

And in that moment, I wished there wasn't a chair.

14
Jimmy Pearson

"Thoonk!!!"

Vincent jumped reflexively, spilling the tray that had been resting on his lap and its contents onto the carpet. The fight he was engrossed in on the TV was turned right up so whatever it was that had just smacked into the window had hit hard enough to pierce through the din of a cheering crowd and the rabid enthusiasm of the commentators.

"Ahhh... Goddamit!"

He slammed the remote down on the couch and looked down at the tangle of ruined pastrami roll and strewn potato crisps lying like a car wreck at his feet.

"You have got to be fucking kidding me"

For a moment he contemplated the possibility of not getting up and investigating the source of the ruckus... Just gathering the remnants of his lunch and letting the match play out. Put whatever the hell was whatever in the "To do" pile for later. They were in the fourth round and the two opponents were in the midst of a frenzied volley of blows and whatever the hell that noise was...Well it could go screw itself. The pause button on the remote could go screw itself too. It was the weekend, he had the house to himself, he'd already paid for the fight and what the hell...Nothing was going to ruin his well earned downtime. Chrissy was out for the day, hitting the streets of Brighton with some girlfriends on her monthly routine clothes shop and cafe crawl. He had taken the weekend off specifically to watch the bout live. This weekend was sacred and nothing...Repeat nothing was going to compromise the sanctity of the occasion.

Except of course an object of unknown origin unexpectedly hurtling into his living room window in the middle of the day.

With a resigned and annoyed sigh he flicked pause on the remote. The two opponents shuddered to a halt and froze awkwardly on the screen locked in an unfulfilled stasis. Vince rose from the chair reluctantly, kicking aside the fallen lap tray with his bare feet.

For a big man he moved pretty lightly. He wasn't overweight by any stretch of the imagination, in fact he was in pretty good shape for a fella of his age and he was always secretly pleased when Chrissy told him he looked younger than his forty eight years. Vincent never had been a vain guy but it made him feel like he was doing something right whenever she mentioned it. The only problem today being was the several cans of beer he had sipped down leading up to and during the fight...And they had started to take a toll. One half of his barely touched roll squelched between the toes of one foot and shards of fried potato crunched beneath the other.

"Shit... Shit... Shit!!!"

Leaving a trail of food debris behind him he crossed the room and threw open the curtains.

Well, thank God for small mercies, at least the glass hadn't cracked. There was however a small spatter of rusty red blood pasted to the window and Vince's initial thought that a bird had come to some kind of mischief was confirmed. He pressed his nose against the cold glass and looked past it and onto the front yard. His breath fogged up the surface and with another pissed off grunt he stepped back and wiped away the obscuring condensation with the sleeve of his bathrobe. Peering out again he surveyed the front yard and the empty driveway. It was bright out there, for all intents and purposes the perfect British Autumn day and if it had not have been for the fight he may just have gathered his fishing gear and transplanted his beer and snacks and sat out on the pier for a few hours.

Almost as to prove a point he caught a fluttering commotion on the grass below...A frantic beating of broken wings in what could only be a death spasm of some unpleasant kind.

"Aww shit," he muttered again. Of course. It was only some dumb bird, a pigeon by the look of it, that had flown like a damn moron straight smack into the glass. Dumb animal or not he couldn't let the stupid creature suffer. He caught another sickly flurry of feathers and wings and he knew that he was going to have to take an extended break from his me-time and take the situation into hand. At least Chrissy wasn't here to see it. She had a soft spot for animals...If a spider crawled into the house she refused to swat it; instead gathering it up gently with a folded piece of paper to be released safe and sound outdoors. Best she

126

not witness what he was about to do...Have to do. Sure it was going to be a mercy killing and obviously the kindest resolution to the problem. He just didn't like her seeing that. Vincent didn't like her seeing him do that kind of thing one little bit. Acts of violence no matter how big sometimes brought up memories...And none of them were pleasant...Well maybe a little pleasant?

She knew as much about his past as she needed and she kinda sorta knew exactly what he had been capable of in a different life a long time ago. Still, even though that book had been closed for over two decades there was no need for her to see him in that antiquated light...Ever. The few stories he had told her about his Jersey days were enough. Even if it was just putting a pathetic pigeon out of its misery by crushing its vertebrae between his thumb and forefinger... Well... He didn't want to paint a portrait of the man he once was and was never to be again.

Stepping onto the front lawn, Vincent drew the gown around him. The sun was trying its best but a strong chill wind was blowing. He half cursed half beer-burped as he realized he had forgotten his slippers but could not be bothered going back inside for them. Just get the job done and over with. He strode as far he could down his drive and then padded across the cool grass, scraping his feet on the way to dislodge the moosh of bread and meat that was stuck between his toes. Lying there on the lawn in a dazed mess was the injured bird, the beating of its broken wings now less frantic and more spasmodic. The wind must have knocked it off course from wherever it was headed; facilitating its fateful meeting with the deadly solid surface of the window. He stood over it and looked down. There was no going back for the poor dumb creature. It was a goner, it just didn't know it and still it flapped uselessly...Maybe even a little more so since it noticed Vince's presence. Bending over he picked the injured bird up as gently as his big meaty hooks would allow. As close to death as it may have been still it fought against his strong fingers. Even though it instinctively sensed its impending mortality still it struggled against the inevitability of its own demise.

"Shhh... Come on now... You ain't helping yourself."

He felt the pigeon's heart pounding through its feathers and for a second felt something that he had not felt since his time working the streets back in the day. There was a measure of pity there...But also tucked away deep in the pit of his gut sang a noticeably audible note of anticipation.

"Poor little bastard...Guess you just picked the wrong day to go out joyridin'."

With an almost insignificant flexing of tendon and muscle he snapped the bird's neck. The breaking cartilage made a decisive crack. It wasn't a loud crack but it made him smile ever so slightly just the same. It made him remember...Remember the night he curb stomped Lenny Rizzo's face into oblivion after that boosted car deal went bad...Or the time he broke every finger on the hands of that little degenerate gambler wiseass Tony Benito for cheating at cards. Didn't matter if it was a stupid bird or an equally stupid human; the sound of breaking bones was all the same.

128

Unique and sweetly satisfying.

The pigeon's body twitched once...Twice...And then slumped limp in his grip.

He didn't realise it but he was grinning.

"huh?!"

Maybe it was the beer...Maybe it was the brief flush of bloodlust...But it was only now as he examined

the dead animal that he noticed the thin little metal cylinder attached by a fine wire to its dangling scrawny leg.

"What the fuck?"

It was a goddamn messenger pigeon.

"Well I'll be damned"

Slamming the front door open Vincent marched through the house and straight into the kitchen where he grabbed some paper towel and lay the bird's stiffening corpse out on the kitchen table. He pulled open a drawer and grabbed out one of Chrissy's extra sharp knives. He knew that would piss her off but he was too charged to care.

With a growing sense of something more than curiosity Vincent picked at the wire with the tip of the knife. It was pretty fiddly work and his patience at this point was non-existent. For a moment he considered how delicate an operation this must be if the bird was still alive and breathing...But good for him it wasn't.

"Ah screw it."

He quit tugging away at the straps and just simply sliced the bird's leg from its body. Blood drained out and soaked into the paper towel as he held the severed limb before his eyes. On closer examination he could see that there was a little screw top lid at the end of the aluminium tube and that his impromptu butchery had been completely unnecessary...But hey, what was done was done. He tugged the cylinder from the bloody stump and dropped the dripping leg unceremoniously next to the rest of the avian remains.

With increasing excitement he unscrewed the cap lid off, tossing it next to the wet mess left on the table. Chrissy would lose her mind if she saw the state of things...And in the kitchen no less! He was grateful once again that she was out till at least five or six. Snapping a wounded pigeon's neck out of mercy was one thing. This gory little extravaganza was entirely another. How many times had he told her..."I'm not THAT guy anymore". Yeah right.

He examined the capsule and could see an intricately rolled up piece of paper housed within its casing so he tapped it out eagerly into his open palm. Very delicately and with careful fingers he unfurled the tiny scroll and held it up for examination. There was writing on it but the text was too small...He squinted hard and still it was just a blurry dyslexic jumble. He needed his glasses.

Running from the kitchen he found his specs sitting where he had left them in the loungeroom. The two boxers remained paused on the TV screen but for the time being Vince had all but forgotten the title fight and he paid the frozen combatants absolutely zero attention as he rushed back to the kitchen.

He stared hard once. Then stared hard again. His eyes narrowed and as the words on the tiny page began to shimmer into focus the colour drained from his face. Shaking his head Vincent felt all the blood drain from his body and his knees melted into soft putty. What the hell was this? What the actual fuck?! His eyes danced over the message one more time and he dropped the piece of paper onto the table where it furled back up and rested almost like a portent of doom next to the dead bird. His knees wobbled again and almost automatically he pulled out a chair from under the table into which he slumped like a deflating balloon. For a big solid guy he suddenly looked very small...Vulnerable even. All the joy derived from this afternoon's unexpected flurry of violence was gone, his face ashen with obvious dread.

He rubbed his eyes hard, trying to erase the words he had just read but it was too late. The pigeon had done its job and delivered its message loud and clear and in goddamn Technicolour.

"They found me. The motherfuckers...They finally found me."

Vincent gazed in daze at table and instead of the mangled remains of the bird all he could see was himself, his body broken, violated beyond repair, one leg now a moist knob of flesh seeping wet ochre in a Rorshach blot onto the bedding of kitchen towel.

"I'm a dead man...I am a fucking dead man walking."

"Vince! Vincent I'm home!"

A windswept Chrissy struggled to keep the front door open against the draft as she bustled through

131

carrying shopping bags and high spirits. Obviously her day trip to the city had been a successful one. She shut the door, locking it behind her and then progressed to the front room. The two fighters were still frozen in place on the television screen and she saw the remains of her partner's lunch left on the floor where they had been dropped hours before. She frowned...A dozen different scenarios crossing her mind at once, none of which were anywhere close to the right one.

"Vince...Baby...Where are you?" She dropped her bags, concern now etched on her pretty face.

"Vincent?!"

"Uuurgh!"

The garbled mumble came from the kitchen. Oh god...He's had a heart attack...A stroke. She ran in the direction of the pained murmur, stopped at the kitchen entrance and screamed.

There was Vince, his head resting on folded arms on the kitchen table; in front of him a half empty bottle of bourbon and a dead pigeon laying in a pool of blood, it's severed leg right next to it. Vincent...Heard the scream and roused awake from his drunken stupor. He raised his head slowly and looked up at her. His eyes were swollen and red with booze haze.

"They found me babe...I don't know how but the cocksuckers finally found me"

Chrissy looked again at the tiny scroll of paper. She squinted to read the words as she mouthed each one silently. She gazed at the paper intensely, reading it over several times before putting it down. The pigeon, its severed legs and the wads of clotted paper towel were now gone...All safely hidden away in a plastic bag tossed outside into the wheely bin. Vince cradled a cup of coffee, sobering up but still sweating profusely. For all intents and purposes he may as well as have had a coronary judging by the state of him. Folding her arms Chrissy glared at him in an incredulous mixture of disbelief and worry.

"Are you sure Vince...Are you certain? It's been 25 years since you left the States for god's sake. Surely you have been off the radar long enough to have been well and truly forgotten by now."

Vince wiped the sweat from his brow and shook his head. "The family... forget? They never forget. Once you're in you are always in...I was a friggin idiot thinking otherwise. I don't how they did it...But they found me"

"And they let you know they found you by sending a carrier pigeon with this stupid damn cryptic message attached...Really. I mean Vince...Carrier pigeon?!"

His patience wearing thin, Vincent stood up from the table and waved his hands in the air in frustration.

"Carrier pigeon...Royal Mail...Strip-o-gram...They'll send the message any way they damn well like.

And trust me...The message has been sent. Look at it. "How vainly we roam" "The bird has flown"...No need to fucking spell it out is there."

He was pacing the room now so Chrissy took his spot at the table. They had been together now for nearly twenty years. She knew his story...At least as much as he had allowed her in on. He hadn't always been Vincent. Once upon a time he had lived in New

133

Jersey and had been involved in things better left unmentioned. She knew that sometime back in the 90s, during the fall of the New York mob and the disintegration of the Gambino crime family a man known as Frankie the Hammer disappeared off the face of the earth and another man...A hardworking, kind and honest Italian American...An average Joe named Vincent immigrated to the UK to start a totally legitimate car refurbishing business. A man named Vincent who she had met on a frosty winter's day sitting in cafe in Brighton and eventually fallen in love with. When he finally began to tell her the truth about his previous life...It didn't matter to her. Somehow those stories did not seem real...The stuff of Martin Scorsese movies and cheap crime novels. And for those twenty years they had been together that's all they had remained to her...

Just stupid stories.

That was up and until she had come home to a mutilated carrier pigeon left strewn on her kitchen table.

"Carrier pigeon...Right...More like a fucking stool pigeon. Metaphor...These guys love their fucking metaphors" Vincent sat back down and looked across the table at her. He loved her, of that there was no doubt. But at this moment she was naïve to the harsh truths of the world. It was one thing her knowing that he had a shady past. It was an entirely other thing living together and sharing a shady present. He reached across the table and took her hands in his.

"Listen babe...I know this a lot to take in. I know...I am having trouble processing it myself. But the fact of

134

the matter is that my goose has been cooked. Somebody somewhere has ratted me out. Maybe it was the London Firm...Maybe a Brighton connection...I got no idea? I don't know who or how but its all right there on that little piece of paper...This bird has flown alright."

She nodded as he spoke, as if she was agreeing with him, but to be honest it was all too big and too much all at once. Her head felt like it was going to pop.

"So if your old family have found you I guess there really is only one question...

What are we going to do about it?"

Vincent smiled and squeezed her hand a little tighter. She couldn't tell if it was to reassure her or just an entirely reflexive gesture. The grey pallor was rapidly draining away from his features and she could see something change in him right before her eyes. His posture was different and something steely was glimmering in the back of his eyes... Something that she had never seen in them before. Or maybe she had but had just never acknowledged it.

"Well baby this is what we are going to do about...You are going to get packed and go visit your mother for a couple of weeks. Tell work that there has been an emergency or whatever... I just need you to get out of town for a while until this thing plays out."

When she first met and dated Vincent all those years back having a sharp looking Italian American boyfriend with a cool accent made her feel special...Even more special when slowly over time he began to drop little nuggets here and there about his less than respectable past. Not only was he dark, big and handsome...But he was dangerous too. That thought had given a her a sharp little thrill every time.

Even though those days were left far behind, once upon a time her man had been a real tough guy doing tough guy things and as mundane and every day as their lives may have become there was that glimmer of something dark and exciting lurking there in the background. To everyone else in town Vincent was that hard working guy who was good with motors and had the cool accent. To her he was her very own wiseguy-goodfella-badass and the fact it was her own little secret from the rest of the world made it all the more sexy. She knew he tried to keep all that gangster stuff away from her as much as possible, but truth known nothing got her wetter than his Robert DeNiro impression.

Right now though, at this very minute it didn't feel sexy. Not one bit. For the first time in their twenty years together she felt fear. Chrissy could feel the shadow of the past swelling up like a wave ready to engulf her.

"And you Vince... What are you going to do?"

Vincent let her hand go, rubbed his chin contemplatively and looked her straight in the eyes.

"What am I gonna do? Well I'll tell you what I ain't gonna do... I ain't gonna run that's for sure.

This particular bird is done roaming in vain. No... No more roaming. This little birdy ain't flying anywhere... This bird is home to fucking roost... This little bird is going to war."

136

Chrissy did just like he told her to. She packed a few bags, rang in sick at the office and got on a train to take her up North to stay with her folks. The entire way to the station Vince's eyes darted left and right... Half steering the car half scanning the landscape for any hidden threats. They hugged on the platform and kissed goodbye. She loved him and she was more scared for him than worried about her own safety. Still, as she boarded the train and waved to him, Chrissy could see the steely glint in his eyes. It was a killer's stare and there was nothing sexually stimulating there at all.

On the way home Vince pulled into the auto-shop. There were a few of his guys there working on various cars in varying states of repair and they all noticed something different in their boss. He wasn't dressed any differently...His hair was the same. It was something in his poise...He was walking with a rigid confidence that none of them had ever noticed before. He took one of the men aside, a young guy with a ponytail...Handed him a wad of notes and then left without announcing his exit.

Back home Vincent was making preparations. Without any panic or urgency he did a sweep of the house, making sure all latches were latched and locks were locked. It was like all the old instincts weren't just rushing back. They were stampeding. Having completed locking down the house he then pulled out a ladder and climbed up into the loft. There left inconspicuously in a corner, hidden away from Chrissy's prying eyes under a pile of boxes and other miscellaneous crap was a hefty tote bag.

137

He pulled the bag from out under the junk and carried it back down and sat it down on the kitchen table. A sliver of a grin crossed his face as he unzipped it and looked down at its contents. With practiced and somewhat eager hands he reached in and removed a Kalishnikov automatic rifle. He smiled at the gun like he was greeting a long lost friend.

"There you are baby"

He reached back into the bag and pulled a handful of magazines...One of which he slammed into the gunstock. Vince slid the hammer back and his eyes literally shone as it clicked back ready to unleash all manner of unholy hell. There was the sound of a parcel sliding through the post slot and though he thought he knew what it was he hefted the gun prepared for anything. It was he thought. The kid at the shop had come through and inside the parcel was a bag full of snow white powder. It had been a long time since he had had a snort but fuck it...If he was going down a trip down memory lane he may as well go the whole enchilada.

He grabbed down a mirror from the bathroom, took it into the kitchen and patted out some crumbly semi-powder onto the smooth surface. With a credit card he cut and divided it into a bunch of lines. Carrying the mirror into the front room he carefully placed it down on the coffee table. He was going to save all that for a bit later. Sitting down on the couch he rested the gun on his lap and picked up the remote. Twenty odd years of anonymity, decades of living a false dream slid away as he sat there waiting for the coming storm. He had never snitched on anyone ever, never flipped for the authorities... When Gotti went down he saw the writing on the wall and he just wanted out. He'd pulled a few strings, flew over to England on a fake passport, started a business, met Chrissy, got married and laid low. Frankie was gone... Nothing but a fever dream. What had emerged had been Vincent and for the longest time that had been just fine and dandy. But somewhere in the back of his mind he knew the past was gonna catch up with. Once a made man always a made man. There was no leaving the life once you were in...God knew he had tried. Still, as content as he had been living the existence of a civilian, there had always been just bubbling under the surface that old fire. That old taste for blood and the streets.

"This bird ain't flying anywhere... It's Hammer Time baby!"

With one hand resting lovingly on the wooden stock of the automatic weapon he picked up the TV remote, hit play and finished watching the fight.

Two blocks down the road from where Frankie the Hammer sat in his darkened room cradling his AK-47 waiting for the wraith of all of Cosa Nostra to rain down on him Wendy Clapham stood in her tidy little backyard going about her everyday chores. She was in her seventies, slightly overweight with dyed hair, lived alone and listened to Daniel Odonell CDs... She had even seen him at the Pavillion at least three or four times now. He was her favourite. Only Shaking Stevens came anywhere close to Daniel. In one hand

139

she held a cup emblazoned with the Union Jack and with the other she tossed seed into the large birdcage that dominated her yard space.

"There you go darlings... There you go. Eat it up and grow strong!"

With each throw of feed the cacophony within the enclosure of beating wings grew more intense as the birds locked inside cooed and shuffled about in competition for the bounty of seeds she offered.

"There you go... Yum yum!"

She paused for a moment. Over the cooing and flapping of feathers she could hear her phone ringing.

With a faffing wave she turned from the cage and shuffled across the yard and into her well kept and tidy little pensioner's bungalow. Mounted just above her back door was a lacquered sign.

"West Sussex Homing Pigeon Club and Society"

As she shuffled across her lounge room she turned down Radio 4 on the stereo (it was nearly The Archers time!) and flumped into her favourite recliner. Her front room was adorned with trophies and on her wall were framed photos...Mostly of her proudly holding pigeons up in the air like a champion formula one driver would brandish a bottle of champagne. The pose was repeated time and time again...The only thing that varied in the images was the bird and her age. She had been racing and training pigeons for years. Putting her feet up on the cushioned poof she reached over to side table and picked up the phone.

"Hello?"

"Hello...Wendy. It's Burt from Shoreham here. How you doing?"

Wendy smiled at the familiar voice.

"Oh hello, Burt. I am good, luv... Still a bit blowy over this side...But I am good. Just feeding the birds as it happens."

"Aww... Sorry to interrupt."

"No dear... That's perfectly alright. Yes that wind is a right nuisance. Hope it all calms down for the race this weekend!"

"Yes... Me too. It would be a shame to have to call it off... Anyway, I was just calling to see if she had arrived yet?"

Wendy shuffled her weight in the chair, trying not to get too comfortable as she would only have to get back up in a minute to make her afternoon pre-Archers cuppa. The birds were going to have to wait for the rest of their feed until after her shows.

"Sorry Burt but no...No sign of her. I know it was only a short course but that wind just came out of nowhere yesterday...Probably blew her off course. Who knows...She'll probably show up some time or another."

There was a short pause on the other end of the line as Burt contemplated the potential loss of his newly trained pedigree bird.

"I hope so Wendy. She was a damn fine Columbinae... A lovely bird. Spent months on her training already. Be a real sad thing if she was lost on her first run."

"Oh don't worry, Burt... I am sure she's fine... Just a little confused by the weather. She knows her way.

So what was the message you sent with her... Anything special?" Even though she was only on the phone she flashed a flirty little smile. She liked Burt. He had the complete Daniel Odonnel back catalogue on CD too.

"Ha... Nothing special. Just the club motto as usual...

In search of true pleasure how vainly we roam,

To hold it for life..."

"We must find it at home... The bird has flown." She completed for him and laughed.

"Well Burt, the bird has flown and now all she has to do is just come home!"

Burt laughed in unison at their shared little in-joke.

"Alright now... My shows are about to start and I need to fix myself a cup of tea and a little slice of cake ready so...I'll see you on the weekend. Don't you worry now. I am sure she will turn up safe and sound. Don't you worry. Bye Burt."

"Bye Wendy"

She put the phone back onto its cradle and groaned a little as she got back out of the chair and hobbled over to her dainty little kitchen to put the kettle on ready for her daily visit to Ambridge.

Just down the street a fourth line of coke was being snorted and a Kalashnikov rifle was being cocked as the UPS man rang the doorbell ready to deliver the Amazon order Chrissy had forgotten to mention.

15
Megan O'Neill

Service assistants come in twos. They help the wealthy into their chairs and wheel them over to a hearty breakfast just across the hall, the general population have to make do with a glitchy automated system and feeding tubes.

Then there's us. We live in the single block of flats in the metropolis of bungalows, the only building accessible solely by the stairs and the only building with neon graffiti spray painted over the side of one of the crumbling walls saying, "Only Well for the attention!". Each day we are startled awake by sirens screaming at us to physically get ourselves up. Complete the jobs the government assigns us to: domestic chores and their outdoor equivalents because, under the able act of twenty forty-two, we aren't mentally capable of doing all that much. However, we can work our way up to the role Domestic Head meaning that, after a successful year of managing everyone else, we can join the ranks of the abilities and become service assistants ourselves.

I walk to the lorry, binbag in hand and toss it into the non-recyclables chute, the smash of glass confirms that the amputee, Parker, in the bungalow opposite has been at it until the early hours again, forcing me to text an A.O.S to one of the senior amp-med officials. Another great start to what will now be a long day of paperwork, travelling up and down temporary ladders, many places aren't accessible nowadays, and confirmations that yes, I am sure about what I heard. I did report the shattering as soon as I heard it. Yes, I have acted in the best interest of the royal dis-jointed society, of which Parker just so happens to be a prominent member of, and no, I don't have any personal agenda.

I don't return to my flat until late evening, by which point I am far too tired to get into my pyjamas let alone cook myself dinner. Half-asleep and half thoroughly annoyed, that's when I see the post-it note hung limply onto the rusted room number. I'm not in the mood to deal with it yet so I yank it from its resting place and consider scrunching it into a tight paper ball, but I stop myself. Nobody has felt the need to leave me a note. In fact, I'm pretty sure the only person who knows about my existence and actually talks to me, excluding the now probably furious Parker, is Blake.

Blake is the guy from the past, salt-of-the-earth kind-of legendary. He's been collecting old two thousand's memorabilia for as long as I've known him and his collection is so extensive that he actually has a special organisation system for it, which not even the brightest members of the G.C.F.D (the general council for disablism) can figure out, hence why he is allowed to keep it and keep collecting. He makes trade off's here, there and everywhere, exchanging precious solid food for these items called CDs and various versions of the ancient device that that really twisted society used to use called a "CD player". This results in him showing up at my door at all hours, insisting that we have dinner together because "he'd just like to catch up with a mate" and not at all because he just gave away a week's worth of pasta to a woman with ADHD who could hook him up with "headphones".

This has one night it would actually be useful to be pestered by him and the hallway remains as silent as it was when I arrived. I pull out my flip phone with my free hand and text:

Blake, were you here before I got back?

Nah mate, I'm actually on my way over now, I made this sick trade with a wheeler. A tin of sardines for a pair of "Heelys". Get this. Shoes. With. Wheels.

Yeah, sure, amazing. Hey there's a note on my door, what's up with that?

Hell if I know man

Hell if you know...I'm calling bullshit on that bro.

Call it all you like; I don't use sticky notes

Well, it says something and I'm too tired to properly read it

If I do you this solid...

No food at the inn tonight mate, do me a solid and get over here

Blake turns up at the door, bright and perky as if he didn't just walk up nine flights of stairs holding the weirdest shoes I've ever had the displeasure of seeing. I hand him the note and he holds it up to the flickering light bulb in the hallway, squinting his eyes he reads: "In search of true pleasure, how vainly you roam, to

145

hold it for life. We must find it at home. The bird has flown." Convinced that I am tripping due to over tiredness, I reach deep into my army trousers, pull out my key and leave Blake standing confused in the hallway.

.   .

One day I will break that siren. I drag myself from under the covers and commando crawl to the kitchen to make breakfast, when I arrive I find Blake sitting at the table eating the last of my powdered eggs on toast with a smug smile on his face.

"Oh come on mate, I've got work today!"

"So do I."

"I'm pretty sure that sitting around waiting for the Gov to give you a better long-term work assignment doesn't count"

"Beats doing whatever the hell it is you waste your time on"

"You can be a real ass, you know that right?"

"Yeah, but would an ass have spent all night trying to figure out what that crazy note meant?"

"But you didn't mate, you wrote it"

"You believe whatever you wanna believe. 'Pleasure, how vainly you roam to hold it for life'…"

"I get to break the rules for once."

"Nah man, I wouldn't just take it like that…"

"That's exactly what it is! You're over-complicating things!"

"But you still don't know who wrote it"

"I see you're still playing dumb"

Blake ignores me as he finishes my food, then gets

up and leaves his dirty plate on the plastic table. I grab my gloves and prepare for another day in paradise.

I'm late. Off to the East side of the city. This is where the true filth lies, it is as if the houses are deliberately built to dismember even the fittest of the physically gifted. They are inhabited by the kind of disablist who would rather shout "Stand against seeing eyes" and die on the cross of their thick blooded backwards beliefs than be nice to a person who's actually doing them a public service, even if it is out of obligation. On my route today, there is an especially vocal individual, a woman seems to have recognised me for some reason and has begun flagging me down. I have no idea if we've met before looks like all the rest of that type in every way, shape and form, except she's wearing 'headphones'.

"Hello, you there! Able boy! Yes, you there! come here able boy! You are the one who underpaid and walked off with a prized possession!"

"I'm sorry Mrs, that ain't me"

"I'm certain it is, you stole my ancestor's shoes!"

"You're thinkin' of someone else, Mrs, maybe someone a little taller with them blue- and purple-coloured streaks in his hair, I don't have those streaks."

"You walking-perfectly people all look and sound the same to me."

"Well, we aren't"

"Yes, of course you don't, you keep telling yourself that," she said with a condescending pat on the shoulder.

At that point, I ease my way out of her reach and collect her rubbish. However, instead of going around the back as I usually would, I go round the front and grab some bottles I had acquired in secret, from the blind cache in the front seat, and chuck them into her bin. The crash is audible from a few streets away.

As I return the bin, tell her "I'm sorry Mrs but I'm going to have to report this as an A.O.S to one of your senior representatives."

"But those are not mine!"

"I'm positive they are, it's okay, Mrs. The seniors can help."

"You obviously planted them there, they were not there before now, I don't touch 'Sangria'!"

"Of course you don't, you keep telling yourself that." The hassle afterwards made the glorious moment of triumph all the more worthwhile.

Lawson, mate. About the other day... just be careful with that note. I'll get ya new eggs. Proper eggs. Just text.

Forget eggs Blake. Tell me next time you promise you'll "pay back later". It has been taken care of for now, but that woman is now def out for blood bro.

Lawson, taken care of? Explain?

Lawson?

Blake and I reluctantly meet at the deserted park out the back of the flats. I really wanted those eggs as it had been quite literally months since I'd eaten a farm fresh runny egg yolk. When we both arrive, through sheer force of habit we take it upon ourselves to sit on the swings the way we have since childhood with Blake on the right side and myself on the left.

"So..."

"Yeah....so"

"How's the whole 'lets break the rules' thing working out for ya Law?"

"It's actually pretty....freedom. Mate, you have to try it sometime."

"Naw, I'm alright. I got mine already. I get to keep the merch and stuff, that's enough for me"

"Yeah, but aint really much is it. Like you're okay to keep all that stuff with them turning a blind eye to it, but let's face it. We both know they aint gonna do that for me, ya know? I want something like that."

"but you had a job longer than I ever had, you got more chance of making Domestic Head this year then I got in my entire lifetime."

"Yeah, mate, but I got stuck working- you chose not to."

"I'm not like you, tho' I couldn't handle all the "get your filthy workin hands off my bin ya able freak," and "lame is legendary" propaganda".

"And you think I can?"

"Na man, I just think you do and will continue to do."

"You sure you didn't write that note?"

"Yeah, no, I'm totally refined enough to write that"

"I knew it!"

"C'mon man, I was being sarcastic."

He hands me the eggs and tells me 'not to do anything stupid', which I say I make no guarantees because we are both technically classed as clinically so.

Blake! Blake!

Blake!

SOS.

Blake!

Pick up the goddamn phone!

....what is it Law? This is an inhuman hour, even for me.

Have you seen the news?

Na, you know I don't watch it.

Okay, you have to start watching it!

No...you can't make me.

They are gonna downgrade us

Downgrade...WAIT WHAT?!

Apparently able people in my job don't 'provide enough of a service to warrant current funding"

I don't even do your job and EVEN I know that most of your day is spent spotting early signs.

I want to quit.

You legally can't

I know, I legally can't! But you would have thought that we would be more valued because there are less of us.

Yeah.

I'm quitting.

Dude, we've just established that you can't.

But the You in the note said I can break rules. So I can.

NOTE. ISN'T. MINE.

Goodnight.

There is no known physical office for able-bodied Government work assignments. A letter tells you what to wear, where to be and when and you follow the instructions down to the very last detail. Domestic Heads control the daily patrol by following the instructions of a letter down to the very last detail. Today I have no letter, just an agenda. I load up with the others as usual and begin the day, but when we get to the first house with the dis-embodied house slogan "formed bodies are fully fugly",

I scatter everything everywhere. Shards of glass, which are only prohibited by the G.C.F.D, spark as the light pounds out of them when they hit the grass. Feeding tube syringes stab the ground like a voodoo doll and I curse them under my breath for how much they've taken over the years. Bloody bandages get caught in the trees the way that we do when they decide to take things too far and claim the treatment only works on able bodies who are Governmentally certified to be unwell enough to need it. I thought I would be satisfied with one house, but the more I think about that note 'how vainly you roam, to hold it for life', the angrier I get with the privileged majority who get to live in those bungalows I so hate.

I remember being taught about the history of the able-bodied people. Society was so perfect until the coming of The Age, when those ill-formed creatures' understood things in a way that we no longer could, built brand new tech that is still believed to have saved millions and learned how to live longer than we did. The civil wars that followed those advancements were so brutal that entire generations were wiped out. The

151

miss-shapen took their places in our houses of parliament and set out to wipe out our customs and traditions. They were the ones who built those impenetrable contraband centres on the edge of the city to wipe the slate clean for dependent masses who were always uncontrollably dancing with the green devil and they were the ones who hired us to do their dirty work because they can't do it themselves in spite of it all.

The more I remember, the more I hate. The more I hate, the more I remember.

Remember my mother clutching her hand as the red river leaked out of her...the suitcase by the front door with the notice of her re-location from ABLE3991 to AMP8556...Blake leading me to his room with the glow in the dark stars blu-tacked to the walls and giving me a half of his chest of draws... Remember going to special school because of new legislation, which barred certain able-bodied kids from entering the regular ones...show up, obey, respect, repeat...sign language being an essential skill to master else you could be prevented from progressing to secondary...teachers are unlikely to know about how to deal with you healthy freaks...Remember that university has the lowest able-bodied intake and the highest drop out rate...no full-bodies allowed...you're not unwell enough to sit here, move down the back...sorry there aren't enough able spaces left on this bus, try the next one...seen and not heard...keep your head down...if they ask you to stop, keep all of your fingers and toes where they can see them...have you seen the news?...able-bodies matter too, I support them, I vote for their candidate....have you seen the news?.. .no, we don't get sirens where we are, that's so weird... HAVE YOU SEEN THE NEWS?!

In the midst of it all, cuffs melt onto my wrists and a hand directs a whisper of a white flag amongst the mass of fallen memories, "Lawson Amber, you are under arrest for destruction of property and self-destruction of the mind".

A few days later, I'm on my way back home when I notice that Parker has finally returned from his stay in the contraband containment centre. It's not just his mind that's become sharper through the clinical purging of any alterations 'the damage' did but he looks significantly less dishevelled than he did when he was 'encouraged' in. As I turn to walk up the driveway, he spots me out of the corner of his eye and points at my forehead like a sniper.

"YOU! WHAT THE HELL DID YOU DO TO ME?!"

He comes charging after me and grabs me by the scruff of my collar.

"Things were Fine Just As They Were", he grips my arms so tight, they start to go stark white.

"Just. As. They. Were", he refuses to let go until the very moment I think my arm is going to go so numb that I'll lose it forever.

"You're not off the hook, I just don't want to be responsible for able scum like you invading our homes," he declares as he spits on the pavement.

He's unknowingly encouraged a new party to join the fight. I make for his prosthetic leg and as it

153

buckles, the back of his fragile head explodes against the gravel like a grenade. At that moment, Blake turns the corner and shoots down a nearby bush in shock. On gathering up what's left of his stomach, he screams "LAWSON WHAT THE FUCK HAVE YOU DONE?!"

"T-t-the note you wrote- a joke...too good a j-joke, eh mate?... Tell me... a-joke?"

"I TOLD YOU I DIDN'T WRITE IT!" He blinds me with the paper as he walks off and it's only then that I see the truth of the matter.

"OH... GOD... oh... God..."

16

Deborah Boys

2.10.21 Started 17.34 p.m. Finished 11.05

"Hi darling, what a week!" So glad you came to meet me I thought, as we found a seat in the micropub. The steam on the windows, turning to droplets as they merged to form rivulets of other people's breath, which became pools on the window ledge. The cosiness of The Anchored and the general bonhomie all round warmed us up to the point we could take our coats off and order our first pint. Zamzama as it happens.

I made sure not to sit too close to the window ledge but enjoyed the Friday feeling of work done and a weekend to look forward to. Even though the weather outside was cold, wet, and miserable with low cloud and rain making the dark night gloomier. The sound of the sea drowned out by the thunderstorm and the lashing rain. Glad we weren't out on the seas tonight. Not like that time when I tried to impress you with a surprise sailing trip.

How was I to know that it would snow. The storm was building, and the slate black sea was being pushed around by the fierce winds and the currents. A merciless night if you had to be out there on it.

Mulling over the message I had received earlier, wondering what it could mean, I brought it up in conversation to gain perspective and because hearing the storm and receiving the message had unsettled me. We spoke quietly about the body that had been washed up on the beach and the fact that the person was wearing clothes from another time. The clothes were well made it seems. Covered buttons, waistcoat and jacket and breaches. Yes breaches. The stockings and shoes were long gone.

The police reported that on examination the person had appeared to drown but other than that there were no marks or identification to suggest who the person was. Perhaps they were someone who had been in a re-enactment group? When the clothes were examined more closely, they were dated as garments made in the 1850s. Sewn inside one of the seams were some coins. Mixed currency coins such as francs, shillings and Portuguese reis which would also suggest 1850 or thereabouts. If the person had been from the 1850s there was no indication that they had deteriorated or been spoiled by the sea or sea creature's partial to flesh. Then, it was a ridiculous notion to think that they could possibly have come from another time and place. Later news said that a coin around the young man's neck had the name 'Lalla Rookh' on it. Another pint please Nigel!

DC seemed to know about the *Lalla Rookh* because as soon as the name was mentioned he became agitated and said that as a hobby historian, as he called me, that perhaps I was out of my depth here. The fact that I was working at the same local police station as he and was party to all the news undiluted, didn't help my fertile imagination, he said, whilst adding that I really should choose when to have these conversations. Slightly unfair I thought. Realising that he may have been a little harsh, he let me explain what I had gleaned so far.

The *Lalla Rookh* was a Barque and East Indiaman of 700 tons, built in the 19th century, to carry cargo from the West Indies and Brazil across the water to England. On a winter's night in November, much like the one we were currently experiencing, a wild storm brewed up causing a maelstrom of heavy rain, high seas, with waves as high as the boat carrying rum and sugar from Brazil. She was blown off course and was almost stranded on the underwater chalk cliffs about 5 miles off Worthing. These underwater cliffs face north and rise up in the water as much as 3 metres with areas of small rocks and sand at their base. *Lalla Rookh* belays its name which comes from a Persian term of endearment meaning 'tulip cheeked'.

The eleven Worthing crew onboard the *Britannia*, a small ferry, bravely went out in the storm. The force of the waves on the deck and the treacherous waters underneath caused the ferry to capsize before the rescue of the passengers of the *Lalla Rookh* could be done. While the *Lalla Rookh* crew were saved and the barque eventually sailed on to London to offload her cargo, the crew of the *Britannia* all drowned attempting the rescue. DC interrupts to tells me that he did know, following this event, records show that the first official lifeboat was commissioned from a boatbuilder in Littlehampton to ensure that Worthing

157

had its first permanent lifeboat because of this terrible tragedy and the tragic loss of life. It was said that 44 children lost their father's that night.

"Captain, the ship isn't going to make it if this storm gets much worse. We are being tossed around like a cork in a bottle. What do you want me to do? If we don't get this coded message off the boat and deliver it to shore, none of what we know, will survive, let alone the cargo and crew of the *Rookh*. The ship's communications have been all but destroyed by the broken mast. We have two options. To put someone in a shuttle and launch it over the side of the ship before the weather gets too much to handle? Our agent on shore will not see our signal as we are not yet close enough, but we can let her know when we use the usual drop box on shore. Or option two. We can use covert signalling by courier bird and pray that the message is delivered as planned? I do think that the weather will put paid to that option though Sir"

"Aye, Aye Captain, we will launch a shuttle. The new communications ensign will be able to manage this. References were excellent, Sir. His name is Hugh Peters. I believe he was placed onboard specifically for this mission, but I can't help thinking that he has some strange ways. Ensign Jacobs said that she overheard him talking to himself. Specifically, into a button on his waistcoat. However, at this point we do not have an alternative so we must rely on the message getting to shore. We can use option two, if that fails.

Captain of *Lalla Rookh*, ledger entry. 30th November 1850 06.00 hours
Position: Latitude: 50.72254683363231
Longitude: -0.3550727381713737

Ensign Jacobs has left the *Lalla Rookh* to take the message to shore to be delivered in confidence and passed on to the King. The consequences of this message not being delivered safely, relies on information that is required to secure the safety of information hidden and which must remain hidden until we are able to act and have the necessary means to respond accordingly in the future.

"DC buy me another pint and you can tell me what you are holding on to when we walk back home. I know that look that you get when something is distracting you". "When I mentioned the *Lalla Rookh*, you nearly jumped out of your skin".

The micropub was emptying by now and not just from the beer we had drunk. The storm had not decreased any for as we got outside, the wind and the rain slashed across our faces. It was sleeting now, and the icy cold ate into my uncovered head and into my teeth. Any warmth that we had gained from the welcome pint and good company, dissipated in the howling wind that ran up the twitten we took, mistakenly thinking it would shelter us a bit more from the elements.

DC always laughs when I say _twitten_. Coming from London, he would say it was an alleyway or smugglers passage. Well, a twitten may well have been a narrow smugglers passage but more than an alleyway, it also makes it quicker to get away from the shoreline when it is cold and blowing a hooley. The prevailing wind tends to be East to West and vice versa so not so good when the winds change and are coming through the South Downs on a Northerly like tonight. Most of the twitters run from the South to the North with some interrupted by an East to West passage.

The age of them lets you know that the construction from mainly flint, pebbles and brick was due to the materials available at the time when commodities were costly to source and transport. Not quite Bungaroosh walls. That is constructed from materials found and put together in a haphazard fashion. The twitten walls are still standing today. The grey, black, white, and brown and uniformity of some of the walls flint pebbles standing magnificent among the narrow passages reveal the workmanship and thought put into constructing them to protect people sheltering and getting quickly to their destination. To get home. It was too cold to talk. We huddled closely together and made our way home in the dark. Even the streetlights were diminished under the fierceness of the storm.

"Ensign Jacobs at your service Sir. Yes, I understand. I will not let you down. I have trained for this moment and been thoroughly briefed." My first thoughts were how to secure the message in case I didn't make it after all. Putting the coins, I had saved into the lining of my waistcoat was an easy task. How would I hide the message in plain site but not let the secret be given up until the right time? The captain was not aware that I was in fact conveying more than one message that dark night.,

As I clambered into the boat, two crewman who had been privately briefed away from the other crew, lowered me into an endless dark, deep sea. Like being lowered into a bottomless inkwell that sees no light of day but throws off a hint of dark indigo hiding in the depths. The sea swirled, lifting, and falling below me. It was hard not to feel anxious. Are not the hours before dawn the darkest hours? The sea felt even deeper under the moonless night, the chill rose up to greet me, and when the boat hit the water with a splash, I never felt more alone or colder.

It was imperative to row the boat away from the larger vessel but the swell that was increasing, kept pushing me towards the ship and I struggled to steer clear. After what seemed like hours but was only minutes, the current helped to pull me away in the direction I believed was the shore. There were no stars and no moon to guide me. The clouds were scudding above, and I now realised that I would be rowing for my life and for the hope of the people that needed the message I carried.

In the near distance I could just see the *Lalla Rookh* and saw that she had anchored away from the shoreline of Worthing at a distance that no one from land would have been able to see. I understand that this worked for dropping off cargo bound for London but separated out to help people locally here. Times were economically hard here since the fishing started to drop off and the towns along the coast relied on the odd bits of bounty that came their way. The captain had a gentleman's agreement with the local great and

161

the good. Rum and sugar always welcomed. He spoke one drunken night about a tomb he had made there on the hill for holding other such things, that he might need in his retirement. I didn't really pay any attention to this and kept myself to myself.

Morning my love. Do you fancy a trip up to High Down Hill today? After yesterday's weather, we can get some exercise and you can tell me about the young man you found on the beach. Only if you want to that is. You were tossing and turning last night a lot so I will understand if you would prefer that we stay at home or we leave it until we go back to work.

High Down Hill it is then. Good. Did you hear that sometime tried to take the lid off that tomb up there? Really weird as I thought it had been empty for years anyway. A Tomb with two purposes, and handy to hide things in. Why would people want to spoil it for everyone by vandalising a piece of our history?

The views from the top of the hill looking down over Worthing and straight out to sea were spectacular. The colours of the sea reflecting the clear, crisp cloudless sky to give way to a horizon filled with white majestic looking wind turbines. I am not a fan myself (no pun intended), but I do understand that our energy does need to be responsibly sourced. The mud on our boots stuck in large clumps as we trudged over the hill to look at the Tomb and the windswept, leafless trees, gnarled by the wind and the rain on the exposed tophill. A place of belonging, where no one belongs.

I prefer an endless horizon full of unimagined possibility. Nothing manmade to interrupt the view or to distract one's daydreaming. Keats put it so eloquently "Ever let thy fancy roam.... Then let winged Fancy wander." Quite the opposite sentiment to the message that was found in a poem found on the young man. He had cleverly sealed it into one of the larger buttons on his breaches. As I was taking the notes from the post-mortem, it was reported that the button top disintegrated and inside was a piece of paper. It was still legible. Maybe forensics would reveal more information about what had happened and who he was.

"DC, what do you think that message means? You like a puzzle. Is it really a poem or is it a secret message? I can't get my head around what he was wearing, the coincidence of the *Lalla Rookh* and the fact that his body was only recovered this week. Is it possible that his body was somehow preserved at sea, and she only gave him up because of the storms we have been having this week? It doesn't explain how he got to be there and how well preserved he is, considering that the body must be 170 years old. Sorry, I didn't mean to bring this up but for some reason I can't stop thinking about him and wondering what was so important that he had to leave a ship that wasn't sinking".

My love, let's talk about it when we go back to work tomorrow? I have a meeting with the coastguard and county archivist and am hoping to know more then. Try not to overthink these things until we have all the facts, he said. Let's enjoy the day, the weather is improving. This walk is lifting my spirits. Sorry if I was a bit down last night. Long shift, dodgy stomach and all that ok.

The storm came out of nowhere. The rising swell had sharply increased, and the boat was becoming more difficult to manage. The wind was howling through the night. The cold rain had turned to sleet. Nothing cuts into a cold body more than icy rain on an exposed skin. My sense of direction was completely out, and the night seemed to be never ending. Rain started to beat down on the deck of the small boat, which was filling up with water quickly, sloshing around my ankles like icy tentacles climbing up my unfeeling legs. If I didn't know better, I would have believed that the captain was trying to kill me. If not the captain, then certainly the elements conspiring to make matchsticks of the boat I was rowing. It became evident that the boat was not going to get me to shore. The *Lalla Rookh* medallion I wore around my neck carried the code to translate the poem. At least that would be found if anything happened to me. I made sure it was well attached and tucked away in my now woefully inadequate clothing. The coins would drag me down as the wind whipped away my oars and the boat gradually started to sink. Whose idea was this to send me back to place a message in this time.

Monday mornings are not my favourite time of the day or of the week. Although today, was an exception, as I was working at my desk, the report sitting there about the body washed up on the beach had clearly been added too. Someone had been busy over the weekend. I think the people who do those antisocial shifts, deserve more recognition than they get. I had done my fair share of nightshifts and didn't miss them at all, that's for sure.

The poem simply read:

In search of true pleasure, how vainly we roam, to hold it for life, we must find it at home. The bird has flown.

Forensics came back on the clothing. It appeared that they were genuinely made in 1845 or thereabouts. The buttons confirming the date with the picture of the King on. Although on closer examination, the King was wearing an ear-ring which seemed odd. A mistake perhaps or an anomaly in the workmanship of it maybe? I don't recall seeing that before.

DC came into the office, smiling at me as he entered. I have some more forensics on the medallion the man was wearing. His name is engraved on it and some numbers in what looks like computer coding. I have been playing around with the words in the poem and the only thing that leaps out at me at this stage is that by using random encrypting the following words stand out more than the others.

In search of true p**lea**sure, how va**in**ly we roam, to **hol**d it for life, we must **find it** at home. The **bird** has **flown**.

It looks like he was carrying two messages.

References

https://www.lookandlearn.com/history-images/U244053/Boat-Catastrophe-and-the-Lalla-Rookh-in-Distress-off-Worthing

https://en.wikipedia.org/wiki/List_of_ships_named_Lalla_Rookh

17
Zaid Sethi
The Bird has Flown

There is something cruel about words. That love is also a word is not enough for my redemption. It is spring. A time of resurrection and I've been three years dead, not three days. It is time.

You'd think this was a love story. In a way it is.

It started with me/us falling in love. Me and Rachel. Can I speak for Rachel? Am I allowed to speak for her? Do I need permission? Her permission, your permission? How angry am I allowed to be? And what about you, will you be angry too or will you grant me absolution? Can you answer the question without knowing what happened? Can you ever know? I'll tell you what I remember, told from my point of view and you can make up your own mind. Think about it before you decide. Take, say, twenty-four hours to make up your mind. That should be enough. Enough to unjumble my narrative so it could be a story told to a stranger in a pub on a blustery spring day like this.

I don't want to lose you. You are an essential part of my telling this story – my audience. Without you what could my story ever be but a forgotten message on a stone in Warwick Gardens, invaded by moss, prey to decay. It was beautiful before it was tarnished blue.

> 'In Search of True Pleasure
> How Vainly We Roam
> To Hold it for Life
> We Must find it at Home'

I left Brighton thinking a change would help. And it did. For a while it distracted me from what I felt.

Feelings, I'm told, are important...How are you feeling? How are you feeling now? As if the only things worth feeling are those which are pleasurable. As if words have the power to transform feelings - an alchemy professed by therapists to pay their mortgages.

I love the sea. I have ever since university brought me to the south coast. The estuary from where I came was kind like my mother. And my dad, like all northern dads, slapped me on the back as I was leaving and told me to go and 'show them down south what we're made of!'

And I did. I took Rachel up to show them my prize. A first and a girl, objects worth gloating over.

'Made it ma! Top of the World!' And I was. *White Heat* was my dad's favourite film and I was built like Cagney.

I worked through uni with dedication. The same dedication I used in winning my prize in the nightclub she walked into where I was with uni friends celebrating the end of exams. Exams gave us purpose, which is what kept us going for the years of loneliness and insecurity we suffered in cycles of time ever since

168

we came to Brighton. The fear of what we were going to do next encouraged our drunkenness. Rachel's gang gave us a new purpose. Something more than the debauchery we fantasised about during earlier revelries. I told them as soon as I saw her that she was mine.

'Arrogant pig!' said Tom.

'You wait and see,' I said.

'I saw you looking as soon as we walked in. I told them you're the one I'm having,' Rachel said, lying in my arms that night.

'Was I worth it?' I asked.

'I'll let you know tomorrow,' she said.

Neither of us needed to wait for tomorrow.

I didn't go home that summer. I found a job at a law firm. Brian worked there too. A Mancunian, but still, from the North, and that mattered! But that Rachel wasn't a Northerner, didn't. Although Mum didn't take to her, they were both relieved she wasn't from London. Like Clare, she came from Worthing, a place we hadn't visited in our three years in Brighton, concentrating on the east coast for our excursions; Eastbourne, Hastings, and up to London when we could afford to be reckless.

Clare moved back home when she broke up with Brian, and I moved there to be with Rachel.

It was hard for me, although it was a lot cheaper to live there than it had been in Brighton. Brighton wasn't home. It never felt like home – a transition, and I thought Worthing would be the same until I took her back to where I belonged. I was arrogant about my possessions.

I found the stone at the bottom of our road a few weeks after we moved in. I took a photograph to show Rachel. She'd never seen it.

'What does it mean?'

'I don't know,' I said. 'Maybe you find TRUE PLEASURE where you belong?'

'And where do you belong?' she asked.

'With you,' I said.

'But you're not happy, here.'

'I'm happy we're together.'

'That's not what I mean. I mean in Worthing. You don't want to live in Worthing for ever, do you?'

'Forever is a long time.'

'Not necessarily.'

'What do you mean?' I asked.

'Forget it,' she said.

'You're acting crazy,' I said, feeling I had to say something. 'We can't decide what we're going to do with the rest of our lives. We don't know what the future holds.'

'That's the problem with you. You never plan for anything!'

But I did. I do. I planned to study law, planned to go to university, planned to become a solicitor, planned to meet someone, get married, have children, and watch my parents grow old.

170

'What do you plan for?' I asked. 'Aren't these the sort of things you think about?'

'No!'

I didn't ask her what she thought.

'Are we having a row?' I said.

'I don't know. What do you think?'

'For God's sake Rachel. Stop being my therapist!'

I can't remember whether this was our first row. Can anyone? Things happen. You only judge after the event. Give them labels to provide context.

She sulked for two days. We always have rows when we think our relationship is strong enough to weather the storm of juvenile behaviour. Being comfortable is when we stop trying, and when we stop trying is when we believe in our invincibility and, at the same time, the vulnerability of the other.

On the first day I ignored her sulking, convinced that I had won, and Rachel needed time to realise the ignominy of her defeat. But she was stronger than I'd anticipated. Her silence on the second day began to worry me.

'Are you OK,' I asked.

She didn't reply. Instead she walked out of our small sitting room. I listened. Perhaps she'd gone to the bathroom, but I didn't hear the bathroom door open and shut, didn't hear the lock on the door which we never used.

I found her sitting on the bed.

'Rachel, please don't. I didn't mean it,' I said, sitting beside her. When she shrugged my arm off her

171

shoulder, I realised I was the one who'd lost. I slept on the sofa.

We made up. I accepted Hull, Mum and Dad and TRUE PLEASURE would have to wait.

'I can't! I'm working!'

'Come on Rachel, just for a long weekend.'

'But it's so far away, and your parents don't like me.'

'Yes, they do.'

'No, they don't.'

Another row. I went without her, but we made up when I got back.

'I'm going to see Clare.'

'God! What is she moaning about now?'

'Why do you hate her so much?'

'I don't hate her.'

'Yes, you do.'

'No, I don't.'

Another row. She went to see moany Clare that evening and I sulked. We made up when she got home.

One day when I got home, she wasn't there.

We'd had another row. A normal row. A row which didn't mean anything. A row which wasted time. I worked late to teach her a lesson. I went home not knowing what to expect but knew we'd make up.

I rang Clare but Rachel wasn't there. She said she

hadn't heard from her. It was too late to call her parents, but I called them anyway.

'Hi,' I said. 'Rachel isn't home yet. I thought she might be with you.'

'No, she isn't. Where is she?'

'I don't know,' I said. 'That's why I'm ringing you!'

'It's late.'

'I know,' I said.

'What have you done?'

'Nothing,' I said.

'Did you have an argument?'

'No,' I said. 'Of course not.'

'Where is she?'

'I don't know,' I said. 'I'm worried.'

They called the police. I was half asleep when I opened the door. They took me down to the station and questioned me for two days. When was the last time I saw her? What was she wearing? What had we talked about? Had this sort of thing happened before? Why hadn't I called them? They said I didn't seem worried enough about someone I professed to love. Maybe I should have cried more, but I had cried enough.

The picnic was Rachel's idea.

Beachy Head has a morbid fascination for those who believe suicide is beyond the realms of possibility. Our lives are like those seagull scavengers who lie and cheat, who scrimp and save, who fight and make-up, who, fearful of their inadequacies learn to live with what they have, who can't afford drugs, for whom alcoholism embodies beers, who turn up to jobs they neither love nor hate. People like us can never imagine jumping off the Golden Gate Bridge. But San Francisco is too far to go when there are so many other places to see, and Beachy Head is just around the corner with near equal fame.

Neither of us ever spoke of suicide. Why would we? We had everything we needed to live out our mundane lives, finding pleasure without the need for kink, looking forward to owning our home by the time we retire and raising 2.3 children which our parents can dote on. We thought the accidental-on-purpose overdoses of celebrities was confirmation of their ingratitude. We are never that ungrateful.

I didn't want to go. I'm sure I didn't. I'm sure I said so. But she insisted. It was a game we played.

'Oh, please, darling. It'll be so much fun.'

And when that wouldn't work...

'You say you love me, but you never do want I want to do. I always do what you want.'

'You'll want moany Clare along.'

'No, I won't ask Clare to come. It'll just be the two of us.'

'But Beachy Head!' I said. I think I said. I'm sure I said. That's what I'd have told the police if they'd asked me. If they'd known. If Rachel had mentioned it to Clare which she obviously didn't. If Rachel had mentioned it to her parents, which she obviously didn't. If she'd mentioned our trip to anyone, which she obviously didn't.

Moany Clare came to get me from the police station. Rachel's parents didn't want to see me. I cried when I got into the car with Clare. Cried on her shoulder with real tears of loss. Moany Clare, who moaned about all the boyfriends she couldn't make, comforted me.

It was a lovely day. We were sick of the wet summer. We deserved the blue cloudless skies. Rachel made me carry the picnic basket for miles. And the blanket too. When I complained. When I said we didn't need privacy, she said she had a surprise for me. When you've been together for three years, sex is never a surprise. When you have a bed, why suffer the inconvenience, the discomfort of outdoor sex? But I didn't say any of it. She was in such a good mood, I played along. Of course, I continued to complain because that's what she expected me to do. The more I'd complain the more she'd make it up to me.

We found our spot. The picnic was more than worth it. Lying on the blanket I watched her look out to sea. I loved her then, radiant as she'd been that evening when I saw her come into the nightclub.

'I love you,' I shouted at the top of my voice.

She turned to me and smiled before she lost her balance, slipped, and fell. I scrambled after her as far as I dared. I didn't hear scream. I looked around, but there was no-one. I sat in silence until it was dark. No suicide patrol found me. I threw the picnic over the cliff and left.

It's been three years. It is time. Rachel has joined the thousands who go missing every year, and Clare doesn't moan any more.

Before we left, I sprayed my final message covering the words on the moss-covered stone. I sprayed it blue.

I never told Clare what I did, but now you know, 'The Bird has Flown'.

18
Amanda Hubbert

Lily needed a break, it had been one hell of a year, she packed her bag and items for the journey into her dads old Allegro. She hoped that it would make it were ever she decided to go.

Sitting in the driver's seat she felt free, she hit the motorway and it was reasonably clear. She opened the window and let the air flow through her hair, she put on her music and sang along as she drove. Lily had no idea where she was going, as soon as she saw a name she liked she would turn off.

Nearly two hours into the drive she started to look for a service station, she needed the ladies badly.

She stopped at Membury services. She parked and found the facilities, now for the hunt for food.

Lily was extremely happy to get a cup of Yorkshire tea and even happier to find some doughnuts. After all calories don't count when you're on holiday, she laughed to herself.

Lily gazed around the services people watching and looking at the posters, her eyes were fixed on a poster for Wales, that's where she should go, she had never been there so this was her chance.

She continued to follow the signs on the M4 and

finally crossed the Prince of Wales bridge, paid the toll and drove into Wales. Now what? Where could she stay?

The rain started to come down, Lily quickly turned the handle to close the window, he right side was quite wet, she pulled into Cardiff Gate services.

On one wall off the restaurant there was a poster of a map of Wales. Perfect Lily, I thought, I will close my eyes and where you finger lands is the place I'm going to stay.

She stood at the poster, eyes closed and finger going round in circles until Lily said to herself stop.

Lily's finger stopped at a town called Angle, so that is where she was going to head for a quiet break by herself.

Still smiling she headed for W.H. Smiths for a meal deal and a map. She sat at the table eating her sandwich and checking on her phone for places to stay in Angle. She found a quiet old farm house in the middle of nowhere that had amazing views over the cliffs. This sounded the prefect palace to relax.

She phoned the number on the website and spoke to a gentleman and booked five nights in the old barn. She ate the rest of her sandwich and put the other items in her bag and headed out to her car. The rain was still coming down but it did not dampen her mood for a break away from it all.

Lily drove for two hours before she arrived at the farm house. It was already 6pm but the weather made it feel even later.

She was tired and just wanted to get her head down, she parked the car. Collected her bag and headed in the direction of the building. The light came on flooding the path, like a moth to a flame she headed to the farm house.

An elderly gentleman greeted her with a smile at the door, he stepped aside to let her in. The building smelt of log fires and large wooden beams ran along the ceiling the entrance hall was vast but welcoming.

Lily could imagine the place in its hay days full of guests and noise, but for now all she saw was 90s magazines on the coffee table gathering dust, dried flowers in the large floor flower pots also gathering dust!

She felt the barn could do with a makeover. She took the key from the gentlemen and headed to her room.

As she entered her room, her breath was taken away: there along the back wall between two large windows was a four-poster bed, with all the drapes, the bed frame was a dark wood that was smooth to touch. Alongside the window hung full length velvet curtains. The room smelt clean and freshly polished, no sign of dust or mould, no musty smell at all.

There was a mahogany coffee table next to a large comfy armchair, perfect for snuggling up in and reading a book. There was also tea and coffee making facilities. Lily was in her element.

She had her own bathroom with a large marbled bath with gold plated feet that sat centre of the room, with sink, toilet and radiator alone the edges. A large window was in the bathroom she just imagined the view she would be able to see when she soaked in the bath tomorrow.

Lily climbed into bed. The sheets were soft against her skin and smelt meadow fresh. The mattress was soft and welcoming, it felt like it was hugging her to sleep. Before long Lily was in a deep sleep.

The sun shone bright the next morning streaming through the windows and waking Lily from her sleep.

Lily headed to the bathroom, with a white fluffy towel over her naked tanned skin, she stood open mouthed as she looked out of the window, it was beautiful, the sun hitting the tops of the cliffs the sea gently hitting the shore line below, she could just make out fishing boats in the distance.

The hills to the left looked so inviting. After breakfast she was going to head into town and get herself some decent walking trainers and explore this area.

The smell of bacon filled the room as she headed downstairs to the dining hall. What was it about bacon that made everyone want to eat it straight away?

As she entered, a gentleman introduced himself as Donald and handed her bacon and toast: "Thought the smell would get you up."

He directed her to the table by the window that had been dressed with a white table cloth, napkin and fresh tea and coffee.

"Thank you so much for breakfast, that bacon was delicious, I must thank the chef."

"You just did," smiled Donald as he cleared the table. "It's just me now since the wife passed away, and

I couldn't keep the staff on any more."

Lily smiled and said she would help him restore the place so he had more guests coming in.

Lilly's day had not gone to plan but she loved every minute of it, Donald reminded her of her late father, they talked about the old days and what he used to do, but now he was getting older he just couldn't do it all, he was thinking of selling up.

Lily went to bed that night thinking about this place and how she had already fallen in love with it and to see it turned into one of those high tech places left her in tears, there must be something she could do. Lily finally fell asleep.

The next morning, she was woken by the sun again and she smiled to herself: "I could get use to this"

This morning, she ate breakfast in the garden and watched the wildlife.

Just as she was about to go in and help Donald, an old balloon fell from the sky with a note attached:

In search of true pleasure,
How vainly we roam,
To hold it for life,
We must give it a home.

As she looked up the birds flew off the grass. Lily know what she had to do, she was going to restore this place and call it home and bring back the guest it once had.

Two years later, Lily had a very busy business. Donald had left everything to her in his will – he sadly passed away six months ago. Lily continued to make the hotel his and, on the wall, hung the message she received that changed her life forever.

19
Estella Rua
Pigeonne

Tourne, tourne, petit moulin.
Frappent, frappent petites mains.
Vole, vole, petit oiseau.
Nage, nage, poisson dans l'eau.
Petit moulin a bien tourné.
Petites mains ont bien frappés.
Petit oiseau a bien volé.
Petit poisson a bien nagé.

Tourne tourne, petit moulin. Alice's umbrella was broken in three places. It spun round like a windmill, triggering the endless loop of her favourite childhood song in her head. She hummed the tune; the simplicity of it gave her the focus she needed. To find shelter. *Vole vole, petit oiseau.* She wrapped her spare trousers around her neck like a scarf in a bid to keep dry and conserve heat. Pools of rain formed in the gutter, threatening to drench her with every passing vehicle. *Nage nage, poisson dans l'eau.*

The rain had reached her calves and feet, intensifying the cold bite of the wind along the front. She never thought she'd be so grateful for a plastic bag, without which her change of clothes would be sodden

183

by now. November was brutal without a duffel coat. Sparse fireworks lit up the gardens by Queens Park. They'd been going for nearly two weeks now, but never really got started. A few of the bigger houses had put on larger displays, the Catherine wheels sneering at Alice as she arranged her possessions in the Wendy house of the children's playground.

She'd found the blanket in a residential dumpster. It was a stiff felt material in royal purple, more like a curtain. Alice was pretty sure it harked back a few decades. When the rain came, the blanket was soon soaked. Alice had been at the food bank when the downpour started. There was no point going back to the park for another broken umbrella and a packet of chocolate biscuits. With any luck, the biscuits would still be in the same spot next time she passed. They were Hobnobs, her favourite since arriving in England. Oaty goodness topped in milk chocolate. She liked the way the word sounded, and her friends at work had teased her about the way she pronounced it. 'Obnobs.

Alice had worked at a soup kitchen back in France. She'd ladled hot broth into polystyrene cups, old stock from a local café that was being phased out. She'd been brushing up her English back then, chatting to one of the volunteers, Jane, who was there in Lyon on sabbatical.

Somehow Alice kept mixing up with the words ladle and cradle. Jane corrected her, which she was grateful for, but she still felt the words were connected, and not just via rhyme. The motion was similar. Ladling and cradling. Completely different words in French, though she would have forgiven somebody English for

184

thinking they'd come from the French. Ladle is *louche*. Cradle is *berceau*.

Berceuse. Lullaby. From the old French word bers, meaning cradle. Alice had moved to Brighton for the work. Almost all the shops in the lanes had displayed little placards advertising seasonal roles. Snoopers' Paradise. Resident Music. The bijou shop selling wooden toys and fancy French brands she wasn't expecting to find.

On first arrival, Alice had endless energy for traipsing up and down the lanes. Down to the sea, back up to her flat share, shuttling past the jewellers and the old cake shop, selling chocolate gateaux as elaborate as the bakeries in Paris.

She was able to juggle several jobs with no fixed abode, at least to start with. There was usually somewhere to stay, if only temporarily. A couch to sleep on, her on-off spot in an illegal flat-share, paid weekly. Sometimes a hostel, if she wanted to actually have a proper conversation with people about something other than whether or not the heating was working. There had been options. She was roaming, but she was happy; before the wind changed and she was stuck like that.

Now Alice had nowhere to go. Nowhere to be. Turn, turn, little windmill. Clap clap, little hands. Fly fly little bird. Swim swim, fish in the water.
Petit moulin a bien tourné. When the shop closed for the second time and Alice pulled her last pint at the Hummingbird, she didn't have the option to go back to

the nest. First of all, that was not what happened in her family. Fledglings did not return. Plus, there was no room. The first time round, she'd slept outdoors without a problem. It was mild enough, and the playgrounds were deserted. Now winter was around the corner, and she saw that help was at hand for people like her. At the food bank, there were leaflets about places available for homeless people in hotels.

She couldn't understand all the instructions and information about the restrictions. Usually, she pretended not to be homeless. There were plenty of people there with a roof over their head. Alice liked that. She imagined their families waiting for them to bring back parcels of sustenance, the animated faces of children as they saw some of the more exciting packets being pulled from the soggy brown paper.

By mid-November, it was proving more and more difficult to pretend she had a home to go to. Her restlessness was obvious. She shifted her weight from one foot to the other like a pregnant woman, in order to keep the blood moving around. The volunteers looked at her as if they wanted to ask her questions, but stopped themselves, not wanting to pry. They asked if she was okay. Yes. She was okay.

Petites mains ont bien frappes. Alice heard the clapping every evening the first time round, usually just before sunset. The saucepans furiously smacked with wooden spoons made her nervous. Now, the nights was almost noiseless. For the first ten days, she'd still been in her unofficial flat-share. She was given a grace period to find an alternative. Enough time for the memory to fade of Halloween displays and sandwich boards advertising pumpkin spice lattes. The bitterness of the autumn season had begun.

Christmas displays hadn't been put up in most of the shops. There hadn't been time before the closures. The window displays along the high street told a sorry tale. Some had been stripped altogether. Others had boxes of tinsel waiting to be put up, when staff returned in December, hopefully. Some of the cafés were still open and already had their specials on the menu, boasting single origin guest beans and creamy, glittery toppings. Alice planned to have one of most decadent coffees on Christmas Eve. Wherever she was staying, she would put aside four pound-coins for the most deluxe drink on the menu. She'd already sealed away two in the loose lining of her trainers.

Each time she found a coin, in a shopping trolley or on the pavement, she thought of the story she'd seen in the British press whilst she was on a pub shift. The pub was only open for outdoor service, and she'd picked up a newspaper left behind by one of the punters. It was about a discovery of over half a million euros' worth of gold in the Jura valley. The treasure had been found in jam jars and in the safe of an old property. She hadn't understood all of it, but Tom had helped her get the gist.

Petit oiseau a bien volé. Alice had well and truly flown, and fallen quite far from the tree. Lyon felt further away than it had ever done before. The story of the gold bullion didn't exactly inspire her with hope, but it helped Alice to think beyond her own circumstances. It

187

was discovered in the house of a rich merchant family with no surviving relatives and would be put into community investments. Once Tom had helped her translate the trickier parts of the article, they'd done the crossword together. It was the first time she'd ever done one in English and she surprised herself by getting some answers that Tom missed.

The little windmill has turned. The little hands have clapped.

Petit poisson a bien nagé. There was almost enough rain to swim in, that was for sure. Alice was given a disposable blue mask and took some cheese and crackers and a bag of apples from the table in the marquee. She'd decided to accept help. There was no way she could survive another night without thermal layers.

There was still some battery left on her phone, which she turned on and off again each evening, checking for emergencies, as if she was able to help. A burden was not something she wanted to be, but she liked to think she might be able to do something if there was a problem with one of her former colleagues at the shop or the pub. She could still go for walks with Tom. He always seemed to like her company, and never commented on the damp smell which she knew lingered on her.

Tom was learning French. She'd never taught anyone before. He misquoted Jacques Prévert at her to make her laugh. *Trois allumettes.* Three matches lit at the bar. As he said the words, he struck matches from a box he kept in the till for lock-ins. Three matches. One to see half a smile, the second to see her roll her eyes, the last to see her wince. For an English person, his pronunciation wasn't bad, and the recital didn't make her cringe at all, even if he did seem to be reciting it to her, about her. She had cleaned the soda stream taps and pretended to be busy. Pretended she didn't approve of his larking around on the shift.

Alice's phone vibrated. Tom had sent something. She fumbled with the screen which was no longer all that sensitive after she'd put a second screen cover on it in a vain attempt to paper over the shards and cracks.

A la recherche du vrai plaisir,
Comme nous errons en vain,
Pour le garder à vie,
Nous devons le trouver à la maison.

It wasn't Prévert, that she was sure of. Alice had studied poetry at high school, like every other teenager in France, much to some of their visible chagrin. Could Tom have written this himself? She put it into Google and got no results, so tried translating it into English.

In search of real pleasure,
As we wander in vain.
To keep it for life,
We have to find him at home.

She could tell it was a poor translation. For starters, it probably should have rhymed. Plus, the gendered "pleasure" made it seem as if the poem was about a lover, but she knew it wasn't. Find <u>him</u> at home. That's where she'd find Tom. At home, gaming or reading or taking photos of his cat.

It sounded like one of the Romantics, maybe. Wordsworth or one of those famous wanderers. Every variation she put into Google returned inconclusive results. Le plaisir. One of the few words that actually sounds better in English. She was touched at the thought that he might have written this for her. Nobody had ever written her poetry before.

She pressed on, walking past the Volk's Electric Railway, remembering better days of dancing to drum and bass well into the morning. The rain had eased off slightly, but the bite was still sharp. She felt it in her chest and her ankles, which threatened to make her fold in on herself spasmodically. She looked up at the empty holiday apartments along the front and wondered if it really was too late for any meaningful change. One light was on, illuminating the middle floor of a Georgian terrace house, split up from its original grandeur into uneven slices. She saw the desirably sparse interior, the lack of personal effects. A single person moved from what looked like a bookcase, to a desk near the window, and sat down, surveying the waves below. It was high tide, and the street signs were rattling their death knell.

The horse has bolted. The camel's back is broken. The bird has flown. Alice tried to think of all the idioms she knew about irreversible change. They kept her amused as she walked against the wind, taking a back road to avoid the worst of the chill factor. Tom's

190

flat was all the way up in Seven Dials. Quite a hike. She felt ridiculous wearing her jogging bottoms as a scarf. Once she got to Tom's, she would put them on over her cords and invite herself in for a shower. It'd be casual. She'd say she had just been for a jog. He'd asked her to come over before. He didn't seem to mind about breaching the rules.

Alice felt less certain. Outside still felt more vulnerable than inside, despite the open air. She scoured the beach for evidence of her happier days here. None. Next to a bin was a bottle of red wine. She'd noticed a lot of unopened alcohol lying around on the streets lately, as if it had been put there as a consolation prize for sleeping rough at the worst of times. Some well-meaning soul, who doesn't like red but had been gifted a case of merlot from the Wine Society by a client, perhaps. Alice saw that the bottle was box-fresh. No finger marks, no streaks of urine. She picked it up, tucking it under her jacket for no particular reason other than the fact it allowed her to feel embraced.

The die is cast. The ship has sailed. The egg is scrambled. A pair of dog-walkers said hello as Alice wove her way up the lanes, past the relatively new Ivy restaurant, past the massive three-storey bookshop and the Jubilee clocktower. The streets were so clean. No vomit. No cigarette butts. Where had everybody gone?

The bridges are burnt. The milk is spilt. The bolt is shot. Alice pushed up Queens Road. Gone were the groups of students with their drinking helmets on. Gone were the lavish outfits and feather boas. The

191

mini-market by the station was a real beacon now, lit up with phosphorescent promises of glossy magazines and factory-sealed confectionery. On the kerb outside, a steel-grey mass writhed and fluttered. A pigeon, with one foot missing and a restless wing. Alice thought of bringing it with her to Tom's. *Surprise! Une pigeonne. Pour dîner.*

Once she'd been on a long drive with Lucien through rural France. They'd been to see a play together, just an amateur production. Lucien had drunk a couple of beers, and on the way back to their apartment, they'd hit an owl. It crashed into the windscreen and bounced across the bonnet, landing with a thud on the road behind them. Alice had made Lucien pull over.

The owl was still warm and still breathing, although the rising and falling of its chest was barely perceptible. She'd put the thought of fleas out of her mind and settled the bird on her lap in the passenger seat, wrapped in her cashmere lilac cardigan, which she'd picked up in a kilogram sale. She'd flicked the radio on to steady her nerves. Classical music wafted in the silence between her and Lucien. Alice had used her free hand to look up the bird rescue centre. There was an emergency number to phone. Without hesitating, she hit *Appelle.*

'I'm sorry. It's almost certain the bird will die. We don't take birds that've been hit by moving vehicles. The survival rate is too low, and we're understaffed. The best thing you can do is put it on the ground, in a park or garden.'

The moving picture of the owl flying around her

192

and Lucien's apartment cut to an image of the bird in the ground. She thanked the volunteer and felt the warmth of the bundle on her lap dissipating. Lucien didn't feel the need to remind her that he'd been happy to leave the bird in the road as a hit-and-run.

The pigeon on the kerb wasn't a creature she felt quite as fondly about, truth be told. She didn't really want to touch it, but equally she didn't think she had the strength to put it out of its misery. She couldn't just leave it there to flap its last flap.

The climb up to Seven Dials was even more arduous with a resistant bird wrapped in the legs of her tracksuit bottoms. So much for pretending to go for a jog. Once again, Alice found herself with a bird in one hand and a phone in the other, as she realised that she still hadn't replied to Tom's message. She hadn't had time to process the meaning of the poem he'd sent. She couldn't figure out if it was a way of showing his affection or whether he was showing off his newfound language skills. No doubt he'd been brushing up his French, watching subtitled films and listening to audio prompts on his furlough hours.

J'arrive. J'ai un cadeau pour toi.

The buzzer at Tom's flat wasn't working, so Alice texted again.

Je suis là.

As Tom opened the door, she pushed the bird into his hands and marched through the flat with purpose, calling out behind her.

'I'm completely soaked. Mind if I have a shower?'

'Erm, Alice. What the - ? Why've you brought a pigeon? Une pigeonnne?'

Tom's flat was warm and well-lit. Alice found everything she needed, including a clean towel, much to her surprise. His shower was housed in an en suite. Alice had to pass through Tom's immaculate bedroom to get to it. She heard the bird flapping around in the lounge as she picked out a Transformers t-shirt from the drawer and a pair of Tom's shorts.

'I think I've fixed her,' Tom said as she came into the room.

'She didn't need fixing, just re-routing.'

Petit oiseau a bien volé. Petit poisson a bien nagé. The little bird has flown. The little fish has swum. Tom opened the living-room window, and cupped Pigeonne in his hands. Alice came to stand next to him as he let her go. Not ceremoniously. No countdown. Just *oup là*. And she was off.

20
Brad Kane

It's better than watching a clock ticking away – 17 coffees and I find myself driving down Chester Meadows in the middle of a heroic thunderstorm, just gone midnight. It gave me the inspiration I couldn't get back home. Four walls and a poster about 'Change' made me want to rip down that very poster and change it for another one. I was cursed by the fact that every ounce of inspiration I sought came from adventure. So, remaining stuck inside those four walls for my next story, would no doubt incite an idea about a killer sofa, which only liked eating yellow cushions, with lilies stitched onto it.

I couldn't help thinking how odd it was that there were no deer along this route. Usually if you found yourself driving along here at this time of night, their bulging eyes would blind your vision as you turn the corner, implanting into your head a quick flash thought of 'Am I going to die today?' And almost certainly on every deer's mind in that scenario. In fact, the very notion of crashing was exactly what my next story needed. A shock factor. Something to make the audience grip the closest thing to them – whether that'd be their partners leg, or their own leg. At the end of the day, nobody wants to read a story about a standard whodunit, where the killer is almost always the one with the most neatly ironed trousers. They want drama, taboos, marital affairs... a brother who's an axe murderer - also booze. That kept me awake during the *'tentacle hours'*, as I liked to call it. No psychical tentacles appear, but it was the time of night when my hands resembled the illusion of a tentacle creature attacking my typewriter, trying to convince me that I needed to scrap my entire third act and re-write it from scratch. The secret bottle of scotch whisky I kept in the glove compartment only come out in special occasions, where my sober brain couldn't think and I needed a quick exit. And this is why I am here, in nature, hoping to avoid the very idea of needing to succumb to that option. Dead... cold... silent... nature.

The thunder clapped, just as my phone started to vibrate.

'Shouldn't you be in bed by now?'

'I could ask you the same thing.' I replied.

Kelly was never keen on my nightly drives. She didn't understand the idea that our home wasn't the most inspiring location to write fictional crime stories. I often found myself booking weekends away at notorious hotels and bed & breakfast's where guests had been murdered or *"gone missing"* to battle my on-going writer's block. Anything to get further away from the poster.

'There's a storm on the way. So, I thought I'd just let you know, before I get a phone call the next morning asking me to identify your body.'

'Well, there's always a chance I'll land flat on my face. Do you think you'd still be able to identify my body then?

'You're hilarious, Harry. I'm in stitches.' Reacting with incredible dryness,

'Anyway... You caught me a tad too late... I am in the storm right now, and it looks... terrific...,' I said worryingly as I leaned over at the sight of two thunderclouds ignite into a menacing bolt.

'Okay. Well, don't die.'

At that very moment I encountered my first deer.

The corner was too sharp for me to gain enough leverage to avoid the crash and these tyres were not the friendliest in unpredictable weather.

I could hear Kelly's voice shouting out from the phone besides me, like a distressed radio beacon operator.

'Harry! Harry!'

'It's okay... It was just a deer.'

'Jesus...' sighing in relief 'see this is *exactly* what I'm talking about... You never listen... if I find you coming back here stinking of --'

'I'm coming home now, alright.' Snapping at her 'I'll just have to chuck it onto the side of the road or something...'

'Fine. Just don't make a racquet when you come in. Some of us have work tomorrow.' Boldly stating, just before hanging up the phone.

Was this not work? I wasn't able to work at home, so what was I to do? Let inspiration hit me in the face as I stared at that god-awful poster for the millionth time. At least I saw a deer. For a moment I was beginning to worry that they had gone extinct and I would never get a chance to see one again.

As I stepped out of the car to take a closer look, the first thing I noticed was how its silk fur shined from the moonlight like a beautiful historical painting. Nature in its truest form. A cold dead stallion. Once full of life exploring the outside freely, now depleted of its energy entirely through one simple collision made by man. One click of my trusty flashlight and I could see its beauty more clearly. It's smooth brown fur, its bold soppy eyes, its ---

'...alive.'

I took a step back, as it wriggled its feet, trying so desperately to gasp for breath. It was not a pretty sight. From seeing such a majestic creature at peace under the smoky moonlight, to then seeing it struggle profoundly and fight for its life, was unbearable. It wasn't in my agenda to put a deer out of its misery tonight, but it was the least I could do after possibly ending its life involuntarily. A couple of light hits with my trusty flashlight didn't seem to do the job, so I had to buck up the courage to take one swift blow and get it over and done with.

I had never seen something fall into the darkness like that before, let alone been the one to send it into the darkness myself. I wonder what it saw when it closed its eyes. Do deer also see their life flash before their eyes? Did it understand the reasoning behind me ending its life, so that it didn't have to suffer in pain? Or did it purely witness me brutally murder it without probable cause? I patted its fur gently and did what I had promised to in my head and grabbed its legs, pulling it towards the side of the road, away from the dangers of any more drivers struggling to keep up with the foggy conditions of these country roads. Noticeably, it seemed rather heavier than I would expect a deer to weigh. Its body dragged itself along the tarmac in an uneven jittery motion. I had never moved a deer's body before, so my experience was very much non-existent in that field, but there did seem to be something---

I knew immediately that something wasn't right. A plot twist? The carcass felt very off... As I swayed it from side to side, I knew what I was dragging along did not in fact resemble the shape, nor embodiment of any deer I was familiar with. What I was holding onto, was not an animal. In fact, I knew exactly what it was, and it hurt me very much to admit it. I didn't want to say or even think about what it really was, I closed my eyes hoping I wasn't right. But, then the smell kicked in. That familiar smell. My knees dropped and I carefully turned over the deer's carcass.

I had not run over a deer. But in fact, a very young girl.

It's hard to say how old she would have been, no younger than ten for sure. Crawled into a ball, wearing a bold white dress with angelic wings proudly attached to her back, all cloaked by the deer's carcass. Maybe, she had used it as a protective layer of clothing to brave herself from the harsh weather conditions? God knows why she had even been walking out here at this time of night in the first place... there wasn't a village for miles. And the direction she seemed to be walking towards, was only going further away from civilisation. Nevertheless, what I had witnessed, and acted upon was beyond comprehendible. All those years researching and writing stories about the most sick and vile killers you could think of, I had never once witnessed something which made me want to eject my entire insides and remap my brain into never even witnessing this particular event - which I still tried to convince myself to being a very horrible nightmare. Eyes wide shut, both on my part and hers, as she rests there peacefully. Much like the deer, she felt nothing. Maybe that's for the best.

Was this the inspiration I was looking for? Did I ask for this? I sought out nature's help and this is what it gave me. A case of manslaughter and 20 years in prison with my name engraved on the prison cell. I've read enough stories to know what happens to these people... Who knows this girl? Who knows I'm here? How many people had seen this little girl before I had brutally murdered her? All these questions were circling my mind and I had absolutely no idea how to answer them.

But, the one question which kept coming back to me was: 'Should I tell Kelly?' The woman whom I trusted most in the world. Would she understand this scenario? Would she believe it? Would this make a good story? It would seem pretty suspicious if the murder suspect wrote down how he killed his victims in his next story and sold it to the publisher, as the investigation was currently on-going... Or maybe that would steer the police off track? Why would a writer write about the girl he just murdered? How soon would the police take to investigate this? Maybe nobody knew this girl? Maybe her parents abandoned her? She did seem to be fleeing away from the villages.

Instead of standing here, waiting for the boys in blue to catch me in the act, I dragged the carcass to the boot of my car. This seemed to be the only option right now. There wasn't any time to stand around waiting for a good hiding spot to get rid of any dead bodies you had laying around in the middle of the countryside. Time is precious, when something uninviting knocks at your door. And I certainly was familiar to this stranger. Although, despite the heavy research I had dived into learning about killer's motives and how they avoided on being caught, their approach to dealing with such matters had not influenced any unethical ways of me getting out of this situation.

Twenty minutes later, I was finishing the last drop of my scotch whisky, cruising down the highway, listening to my *'Happy Playlist',* which Kelly had made for me for my last birthday. I tried to drown out my thoughts with George Harrison's voice, but the thoughts kept coming back to me. Was the boot of my car making too much noise? Did I lock it properly? Would the blood stains leak out it onto the road and leave a trail from the crime scene to wherever I planned on going with the evidence? The volume was on max.

Not to mention the several alibis flying around in my head as to why I had been gone for so long. The car was of course an absolute goner. So what would I say to Kelly that would explain me coming home by foot at

4 in the morning? A hijacking? Something probably quite hard to believe in the quiet Irish countryside, but not entirely impossible. The Moors murders seemed like an unlikely location, but made national headlines.

Then, the phone rang.

Should I answer it? I knew exactly who it was. My first instinct was to smash it. Then I thought how suspicious that would look from her perspective. So, without contemplating on it too much, I let it go to voicemail, then promptly smashed it with my trusty flashlight, after the call had ended.

Why was I not writing any of this down? If I just change the names...location... and time period... clear any known association between me and the victim... Ignore the flashing blue lights, it's just a deer.

'Oh, wait.'

This was not a coincidence. Police cars don't cruise down here for no apparent reason. It was quiet enough for me to run over the girl and not be seen. This is the countryside. If you *don't* see anybody around, then chances are that there *isn't* anybody around.

Here's another thought. No matter what I do, they will catch me. They're not racing towards me to have a friendly chat. And they've been drawn attention to the car for two reasons; either I didn't clear up all of the blood stains, or the trunk is wide open with enough evidence to show for them to put me away and throw away the key. I sat on this thought for a moment as my left foot tickled the brakes, thinking I had two options here. Either way could end up not how I wanted it to. It was a gamble. Then, I realised that there was a third option available.

The brakes slammed hard. I peered through my rear view mirror and saw the police car abruptly stop behind me in the nick of time. Taken off guard by the sudden stop, one solitary police officer steps out with an iron fist and tight-fisted expression on his face, implying: *'I'm going to make your life a living nightmare'*.

He made his way towards me and I rolled down the window gently. Before I could get a word in, he initiated the confrontation.

'Having a nice evening, sir?' he barks rudely.

'I'd say it's going okay... just having a relaxing drive...'

'Just a relaxing... And have you been drinking, sir?'

'I have not, sir.'

'Are you lying to me?'

We shared a moment of intensity. Much the same way a father would share eye contact with his son after finding out that he cheated on his last Maths test. The officer didn't seem to be able to blink, which made me incredibly uncomfortable, so I panicked and pressed down on the accelerator. I pumped the music back on, as I tried to convince myself that this was the best solution I had for the current situation. Then, I panicked again, thinking about the car's shoddy acceleration, and realised option two was an idea dead in the water, so slammed down onto the brakes once again.

I started to whistle *'All Things Must Pass'*, as I saw the police officer throw his sunglasses on the floor in a suit of rage and march towards my window once more.

'I'm going to make your life a living nightmare.' he

calmly said out of breath.

I looked up at him, as he forced me out of the passenger seat of the car.

'Easy now!' I preached.

The officer approached my face incredibly close, face red as the devil himself.

'Oh, I'll tell you what's easy... Figuring out what to do with people like you! Turn around, sonny.'

Out of breath, I did as he said, whilst fixating my eyes on the boot of the car.

'The reason I pulled you over... was because you were swerving around like you owned the damn road! Have you not seen the storm out here?'

'I know... beautiful, ain't it?'

The officer pressed his baton against my chest firmly impatiently.

'Do I even need to bother asking ya' for your licence or should I just throw ya' into the police car right now?'

My face was glued to the backseat window of my car as I muttered out that it was in the glove compartment.

'Well, that's handy now isn't it... Don't expect me to reach in for ya. I know what you'd do with me back turned...'

I was beginning to think that maybe he wouldn't need to check the boot and he might just let me off with being under the influence. Maybe he'd had a bad day and my childish attempt at resisting arrest got to him.

As I reached into the glove compartment to take out my wallet, I caught my trusty flashlight in the corner of my eye and I began to think that maybe option three was still a possibility.

'Why the interest in the boot of your car?' he called out from the distance.

My heart begun to race quicker than it had ever done before.

'I'm sorry?'

'I've seen ya'... You hadn't managed to set your eyes off the damn thing... is this something I should... investigate, eh fella?

Was this a time to bring out the trusty flashlight?

Then my brain started to reboot.

'I just had a paint job done, and I didn't like how they did the boot... Looks a bit shoddy if I'm honest...

The officer takes a good look at the car, suspicious of his response. His eye gaze up and down at the paint marks from the wheel arch to the roof of the car.

'Looks like the whole car's shoddy, if I'm honest with ya' mate...'

'Yeah, well who has time to clean these days, eh?' laughing it off lightly.

As I stared him dead in the eye, a large part of me knew that he knew that I was lying straight to his face. But that other slim chance still managed to maintain my confidence to not give in to the fact that I had just murdered a little child with my car.

'Okay, then.' The officer said unconvincingly, taking one last look at the boot of the car.

For a moment I thought I was clear. Then, as I heard his footsteps walk away, he shouted out one more time.

'Hang on a minute, mate... What's this? Blood?'

Hello, trusty flashlight.

It took a good few attempts to knock him cold out, but the flashlight remained working and surprisingly very much intact. The officer's body was light, so maybe there was a chance he would also be able to fit inside the boot. From my latest research, looking at the North Dakota serial killer James Pope, he managed to comfortably fit four of his victims into the trunk of his car and drive down to Mexico with his wife and kids to live a new life in peace and harmony. That however I knew was not an option for me, as I knew that Kelly would leave me if she could see me right now.

The boot opened wide and there was yet another plot twist.

No deer carcass. No little girl. In fact the boot was cleaner than I had ever seen it before. All that remained was a little pair of angel wings and a note:

"In search of true pleasure, how vainly we roam, to hold it for life, we must find it at home. The Bird has flown."

This was far beyond my mind could begin to comprehend. Someone was playing mind games with me here. Was I being followed? Was there a witness to the murder, who had been following me the entire time, leaving a treasure trail for me to follow? Did the little girl escape, maybe? Whether it was her or not who had left the note, someone out there knew what I had done. But rather than fleeing the scene without a trace, they seemed to have found the humour in entertaining the events I have had to witness.

As I hunched the dead policeman by my feet into the boot of the car, I began to regret smashing my phone. What would Kelly think of all this? Would she leave me? Or would she see the error of my ways? How much can you love someone, before you realise that some decisions they make may seem unjustified or selfish? I could have very easily done the honourable thing and claimed ignorance to the fact that I had run over nothing but an innocent deer and turned myself in for manslaughter. But, the exacerbation of the events leading to a now dead police officer lying in the trunk of my car, and a missing girl which I had attempted to murder – who is most definitely finding her way to the nearest village, where they would investigate and very likely identify me as the suspect, seemed to be a scenario I would inevitably never escape from. I know how these things end up resolving themselves. Even the most intelligent killers slip up some time. You can never be perfect at what you do. I'm a writer not an actor. I'm sure even a killer would suffer from some kind of equivalent of writer's block, where they lack the motif to fulfil their desires. Where did they find their inspiration?

I didn't know where I was driving, or why I was still driving with the dead body of a police officer in the boot of my car, but my eyes were fixated on the rear view mirror observing the boot meticulously. I must have driven past miles of cliff tops, without seeing a single soul in sight. No human, nor animal to be seen. I could commit another murder if I really wanted to. But I would need to make adequate space for a second body in the boot, of course. If I just pulled over and dumped the body over the cliffs, it would all be so simple. But then, there's the elephant in the room of course. Who's to know that if I did stop on the cliff top and open the boot, that there would still be a body in there? Did I even remember a police car in the first place? As my eyes remained fixated on the rear view mirror, I realised that curiosity beat the best of me, so I slammed on the brakes once again.

Before I clutched open the boot of the car, I glanced down at my bloody hands. Still dripping wet. How could it be that the blood had not dried out yet from a murder I had committed 2 hours ago? The steering wheel, covered in fresh blood, dripping onto the driver's seat, every counting second. Then, I began to question 'What would I achieve from opening the boot?' What am I expecting to see? What do I *not* want to see? My hands gripped onto the handle and the thoughts went away.

Although, even with an incredible amount of force, the boot refused to pull open. Not locked shut, but what seemed to be glued shut with such pressure, not even a crowbar could break the mould. Nothing made sense. And as soon as I thought that, that statement had never been so literal, when a stream of blood begun to unexpectedly ooze out of a slim crevice within the boot, creating a bright red puddle at my feet. I had no reaction, but to stand there like a deer in the headlights, witnessing this bizarre explanation. The more I attempted to force the boot open, the stronger the surge of blood became, creating more crevices and entry holes for it to shoot out of.

Impossible to get a sturdy grip of the handle, I couldn't see myself progress any further in this struggle, so I hopped back in the car.

I had absolutely no idea where I was driving towards, but as far as I knew I couldn't keep my eyes off of the rear view mirror, showing a clear view of gallons of blood ejecting out of the boot of my car, leaving a clear trail for even the most unintelligible individual to figure out where the source was coming from.

I tore my way through the country roads, passing the first car I had witnessed since my encounter with the police officer. I didn't think anything of it. Much so, I didn't think anything of the fact that, I found myself entering a local village, which obviously turned heads. Every local peered out of their windows as the streets became flooded with rivers of human blood. Some prayed, some hid inside their homes, whereas I; I found myself even more surprised with the fact that the interior of my car was now filling up with gallons of blood. I began to lose control of the car's mechanic and start to drift in the pool surrounding me. I didn't think for a moment for fighting. I just floated there, knowing that my time had come. The final act to my story.

21

Kathryn Andrews

There's a sense that every pigeon possesses – a way for them to find home, even when they're taken far, far away from it. In later years, humans name it magnetoreception, the ability to sense the magnetic fields of the Earth.

Now, however, several thousand years before human science even conceives of magnets, Dances-With-Wind ruffles her wings, and listens to a message drifting across those same magnetic fields.

It doesn't matter where the message came from, or who sent it. What matters is the words, and the meanings behind them.

In search of true pleasure
How vainly we roam
To hold it for life
We must find it at home
(The bird has flown)

Dances-With-Wind considers the words, turns them over in her head. Croons softly to herself in thought.

Not all of the words are ones she recognises. The

humans who care for her and her flock speak to each other, but not to them; though she listens, she can only recall those words she hears often. *Bird* and *flown* are two such words, and that is what convinces her.

The message was not a coincidence. That it came to her, to Dances-With-Wind, here at this moment – it was meant for her, or at least for one like her. Why else would it address them so? They are birds, and they have flown, many times – the whole flock, alone and together, have flown back to their hatching-place, and then woken to find themselves elsewhere again.

And if the message is for them, then it must be understood. Not just by Dances-With-Wind, but by the entire flock. Dances-With-Wind has seen humans working late into the night to decipher the papers she brings; she knows the importance of knowing.

So Dances-With-Wind coos the words to her nearest flock-mate, who passes them on, and so forth until the whole flock is crooning to each other, voices mixing in repetition and echo.

When she flies home, when she is taken to other roosts, Dances-With-Wind does it again. This is something greater than her, than her flock – if sharing it helps the message to be understood, then it must be done.

And each squab she raises, she shares the message with, ensuring that each one knows it before they are out of the nest. For even if her time cannot understand the words, the future may be able to.

Thousands of years and over two hundred generations of pigeons later, the many-times-great-granddaughter

211

of Dances-With-Wind launches from a human hand. Her wings scoop the air behind her, until she catches a thermal high above the ground and settles into easy flight.

Her name is Fellflight, for how her first flight took place. She fell from the nest, too early to truly be called a fledgling, and caught herself moments before she struck the ground. At the time, of course, she flew only a length or two before flapping onto the ground. But she flew, earlier than any other in her flock, and now she flies faster than any of them, too.

Just like her ancestors before her, Fellflight knows the words passed down from Dances-With-Wind. She reminds herself of them now, as she wings her way towards home, message-tube clipped to her leg:

The search for truth, pleasure
How vainly we roam!
That hold on your life
We must find our way home
(The bird has flown)

Fellflight considers herself something of a philosopher, as the humans call it. She was born in an excellent time for it; the message she carries now is of the victors of the great games at Olympia. And the humans around her all talk as much of philosophy as they do of the games, or of statecraft.

Fellflight, then, has given a great deal of thought to the message in her four years of life thus far. There are the old interpretations of it to consider, of course – Diver's argument that the words mean pigeons should hide home, leave the roost only when humans need it; Lost-Claw's belief that it suggests nothing more or less than that pleasure must be found at home, not out in the winds.

But Fellflight considers herself to be something of a maverick when it comes to the message, to an understanding of it. She twists in the air, soaring over a startled gull, as she contemplates.

The first line she thinks so clear that it stuns her how no others see it. She searches for the truth, as all who think on the message do – and the message itself tells them that there is pleasure in it, that the search itself is to be enjoyed. And yet, most contemporary understandings of the message seem to ignore that possibility entirely! Fellflight cannot understand it. No matter how she debates with her flock-mates, it seems that they're unable to see her perspective.

Fellflight snaps her beak in annoyance at the thought. Perhaps she should turn her attention instead to another part of the message, if they will not listen to her interpretation of the first line. This journey should certainly give her time to consider it. Perhaps - yes.

The final line, one that few philosophers have devoted much attention to. It seems obvious, after all - and hadn't Dances-With-Wind interpreted it herself, on the same day she heard the message? *The bird has flown.* It means them, of course, all pigeons. An indicator of who the message is meant for.

But what if it were *more*?

A metaphor, perhaps. The words saying one thing, and yet meaning something else. It was generally accepted that this was the case for the rest of the message, so why not that final line?

Fear, Fellflight suspects. Fear of contradicting Dances-With-Winds, of imposing one's own interpretation upon the only line which their venerated ancestor had chosen to explain.

But Fellflight does not fear disagreement. She respects her ancestors, of course - but hadn't Dances-With-Winds herself expressed the wish that future generations might better understand the message? How could that be anything other than an *invitation* to analyse it?

What she still lacks, though, is an idea. A spark of comprehension, an epiphany. The last line could be a metaphor - and? That alone is hardly anything new. It certainly won't get far in any debate, and Fellflight refuses to look like a fool.

Think, she tells herself. More than two-thirds of the journey is gone now, landscape vanishing beneath and behind her whilst she flew, too distracted to notice the time passing. If she has nothing new to bring when she reaches her home flock, she will have to simply remain silent.

A metaphor - but for what? It seems so obvious that the bird should be *them*, for isn't it true that to be a pigeon is to be the purest form of what humans call *bird*? Raptors, gulls, all other birds are below them, for none of *them* have heard the message. None of *them* are enlightened.

Unless... Could the bird be the message itself? What if the final line had never been meant to be part of that message at all? No pigeon knew who had sent the message, nor where it had come from, and Fellflight doubted that they would ever know. But it must have been sent by *someone*, and perhaps that someone had never intended to include that last line. Maybe it had just been an aside - *the bird has flown*, the message has been sent.

Fellflight paused, just for a moment. What she was thinking now - it went beyond simply maverick philosophy. It bordered almost on heresy. But if it were true... It could change their understanding of the message forever.

As Fellflight began her descent towards the city of her hatching, she knew that, no matter the consequences, she could not stay silent about this. She would speak her truth, make her argument - and let the fallout come as it may.

Another hundred generations or so pass, by human measurements perhaps fifteen hundred years. In France, a young pigeon, barely fledged, goes by the name of Grey-Pinion, for fairly obvious reasons.

Grey-Pinion is not a philosopher like the Fellflight before him. Grey-Pinion, in fact, wants as little to do with interpretation of the Message as possible. He learns what he is told by his parents and by elders in his flock, and he does not question it. Grey-Pinion is far more focused on other things. Things like the siege he is about to be sent into.

Pigeons don't tend to follow human politics very closely. They're far too occupied with their own politics, particularly since the Schism. (Fellflight's words, so long ago, had far more of an effect than even she had expected.) Grey-Pinion, though, has always been interested in the goings-on around him, ever since he was old enough to begin to understand human speech.

And so it was Grey-Pinion who had realised that the humans were about to go to war, and Grey-Pinion who had told the rest of his flock as much. It was Grey-Pinion, too, who had been taken from his home roost in the dead of night, along with a dozen or so others, and smuggled through the air in some kind of human device. Personally, Grey-Pinion thought, and still thinks, that it would have been far more efficient to let him and the others fly out of the city themselves; but it isn't his place to argue with the humans, even if they could have understood him.

Unfortunately for Grey-Pinion, the roost where he and his flock-mates have been temporarily brought is already occupied. And occupied by those who inform them, without hesitation, that in *this* roost they follow the interpretation of Fellflight, *not* older false beliefs.

Some of Grey-Pinion's flock-mates argue; Grey-Pinion himself does precisely what he's always done. He keeps quiet, and waits to be brought out, to fly back to the human city of his birth.

After all, he reflects, why should the words of the Message have to *mean* anything? Why can't they simply be taken at their face value?

They search for truth, pleasure
Yet vainly they roam
To hold on to life
We must hold to our homes

216

(The bird has flown)

Grey-Pinion thinks of the Message even as the human ties a message-tube to his leg with careful hands. *Hold to our homes*. That is all Grey-Pinion has ever cared to do.

Only a little while later, and not so far away in Germany, a pair of pigeons nuzzle together in their roost as they fall asleep.

One is named Dawn-Eye, for the unusual shifting shades of red and gold within her eyes; the other, her mate, is named Short-Wing, for the accident that had foreshortened his left wing early in life.

Both have duties to which they will return in the morning. And both know the Message, though their own understandings of it differ. Not enough to split them, they will not be a microcosm of the Schism that had rent apart pigeon society so long ago; but just enough to allow for some healthy debate.

For both originate from different home roosts, though most of their time now is spent here in the German town of Kronberg. Dawn-Eye was born in Falkenstein, not far away, and still returns there often, delivering precious pharmaceutical parcels at the order of one Julius Neubronner. Short-Wing, however, was born in Kronberg itself, and plays a different role. Julius Neubronner is not interested only in pigeon-delivered prescriptions, but also in something he names pigeon photography - unique, revolutionary, he calls it. And so each day, whilst Short-Wing is released elsewhere, camera tied around him, Dawn-Eye is loaded with medicines and released to fly back to Falkenstein.

But their home roosts are relevant not only because of their duties, but because of the Message.

It has been almost five thousand years and over three hundred generations since the Message first drifted into Dances-With-Wind's brain, carried there by the currents of the Earth's magnetic field, so the tale goes. In those years and generations, there has been more than enough time for the Message to change, to mutate, although none know for sure how much it might have changed from the original. In fact, until Dawn-Eye and Short-Wing met, neither knew that the Message might have changed at all; and it took a great deal of discussion before either of them could accept that.

For the Message passed down by Dawn-Eye's parents and elders in Falkenstein and the Message passed down by Short-Wing's parents and elders in Kronberg, towns less than ten minutes' flight apart, are different.

The differences are not huge; it is still recognisable as essentially the same Message. But they do differ; and this was, and remains, a source of great consternation for both Dawn-Eye's home roost in Falkenstein and Short-Wing's home roost in Kronberg, as well as any other roosts they visit.

The Message taught to Dawn-Eye was this:

They search for true pleasure
How vainly they roam!

218

To find it in life
We must hold on to home.
(The bird has flown.)

And the Message taught to Short-Wing was this:

We search out true pleasure
Yet vainly we roam
To find it in life
We must hold to our homes
(The bird has flown.)

The meaning of the words has become less important than the differences between the Messages, to many. For, without realising, Dawn-Eye and Short-Wing had set many philosopigeons aflutter with their revelation. A roost's understanding of the Message tends to be a private thing, to avoid a repeat of the Fellflight Schism; it is rare for pigeons to share the words of the Message itself. And so none knew how long such differences might have been ongoing. Had the words differed since after the Schism? Before? Had they even diverged only shortly after Dances-With-Wind had first shared it with others? None knew, none could say, and attempts to trace it were often stymied by the reluctance of roosts to share their own knowledge of the Message with outsiders.

Dawn-Eye and Short-Wing, however, cared little for this. They knew their jobs, and were proud of them. Dawn-Eye recognised and valued the relief and joy she saw on the faces of the humans to whom she brought medicine, and the humans those humans then

219

dispensed the medicines to. And Short-Wing loved the awe and wonder expressed by those who saw the photographs he took, the views from high above the Earth that were so familiar to pigeons, but unreachable to humans.

The only issue that had arisen, and still arose, was the ongoing debate about which version of the Message they would teach to their children.

Across the sea, some decades later, a pigeon goes not by a description-name, but by the name chosen for her by her human handlers. She is Mary-of-Exeter, and there is war in Britain.

Mary-of-Exeter is well-known amongst both her own roost and others, although whether she is considered famous or notorious tends to vary depending upon the place. Once, say the histories, pigeons did not follow the politics of their human keepers. At some point (around the time of Grey-Pinion, in fact) this changed; now to be, for example, a British pigeon entering a German roost would be the height of foolishness.

So Mary-of-Exeter's job is dangerous, even potentially deadly at times. Already she has been attacked once by hawks, barely escaping them with her life. But she had delivered her letter, she had fulfilled her duty, and for Mary-of-Exeter, that is enough.

The hawks, of course, do not know the Message. No birds other than pigeons do; that is a truth that has held since the very beginning. Sometimes, Mary-of-Exeter wonders what might be, might have been, if this were not the case; if the Message were shared with others. But then she dismisses that thought. After all, the shared Message has not prevented pigeons from being divided along the lines of human politics. And even before that, the shared Message did not prevent the Fellflight Schism, nor did it prevent the Message from changing, diverging, within different roosts.

Divergence is a well-known phenomenon, now. Mary-of-Exeter makes a habit of learning what Messages she can, when she is stationed at different roosts. So far, she has only found Messages which diverge in a word or two, but then she has not travelled far beyond her home-roost, and ever since it was first realised that the Message had changed, nearby roosts have made far more of an effort to ensure that the Message remains the same from roost to roost. It is their duty, after all, to preserve Dances-With-Wind's original Message, as much as they are able to.

To that end, roosts will share their Message, now. And so Mary-of-Exeter repeats it to herself, even as she prepares to be sent out again across the sea.

In search for true pleasure
How vainly we roam
To have it for life
We must have it at home
(The bird has flown)

Mary-of-Exeter has her pleasure at home. The roost is comfortable, there is always plenty to eat, and her human is kind and cares for them all well.

And yet at times, when the adrenaline flares and

the wind whips through her wings, and she cannot imagine being anywhere else... At those times, she wonders if she is truly adhering to the tenets of the Message. For she does not roam in vain, and she has no need to search for pleasure, not when she can swoop on the thermal currents of the air, outspeeding hawks, gulls, even human planes at times. She has her pleasure at home, yes - but Mary-of-Exeter, though she admits it only to herself, takes far more joy in her flight than anywhere else.

A human lifetime, and five generations of pigeons, have passed. No longer do pigeons live in roosts, cared for by humans. Their value was lost to most as human technology progressed, as humans developed the capability to send messages in a blink, far faster and more securely and more reliably than any bird might carry them. Now, flocks roam the streets of human cities. They still share the Message, of course, but now it is viewed more as a warning, or an expression of grief.

In search of true pleasure
How vainly we roam
To have a whole life
We must have our own home
(The bird has flown)

The flocks that wander the cities have homes, true, but they are nothing compared to the stories which some elders still tell. Of roosts and lofts, and humans who cater to their every need. Of a time when there was no need to scrabble on the ground for scraps. Of a time when pigeons were lauded for their bravery and their speed, rewarded for it.

But the pigeon we find now is not one of the feral flock-members who roam the city streets. His name is Rory, and he is a highly trained, specialised racing pigeon. For him, life has changed little from the pigeons of old; he still flies at the request of his human, although he does not carry messages.

Until today.

Today, an experiment is taking place.

The item tied to Rory's leg bears little resemblance to the message-tubes that were once used. It is what the humans call a memory card; a new way to contain and transmit information, in far greater amounts at a much smaller size than ever before.

Rory has paid enough attention to the words of his human to have something of an understanding of the purpose of this. They are on a farm, interesting enough in itself for Rory, who has never visited one before, having spent most of his life either within his home-roost or at races. And the point, so far as Rory can understand it, is to prove that a pigeon can carry this information far more quickly than human technology might be able to.

Rory fully intends to live up to the challenge. *His* home-roost still holds to the old knowledge of the Message, with much the same wording as Mary-of-Exeter knew some generations ago; he knows his duty, thrives on it. Racing is something Rory enjoys well enough, but he has always dreamed of doing what his ancestors did before him, of carrying vital information, of being - in short - a hero.

Proving a point about poor internet speeds isn't quite as heroic as he might have liked, but Rory will take it.

And, sure enough, a little over an hour after beginning his flight, Rory swoops down to deliver his message - well ahead of the human technology, which he later learns had failed halfway through.

Rory preens.

And now, at last, we come back to where it all began.

In a town in England called Worthing, on the south-east coast, there is a slab in the pavement a little off the beaten track. The slab has words engraved in it.

They say:

In search of true pleasure
How vainly we roam
To hold it for life
We must find it at home

There is only one line missing; and that missing line is why the pigeons of Worthing are firmly on the side of the Fellflight Hypothesis, never mind that it alienates them from many other flocks. Because of this, the pigeons of Worthing also have something of a reputation for being... eccentric.

Cloud-Down, born and raised in Worthing, is no exception.

She is pure white, an unusual genetic mutation from whence her name originates. And she tends to alternate her time between examining the slab with the Message engraved on it, wandering the town, and debating furiously with her flock-mates at the Warrior Birds memorial in Beach House Park. The memorial has become something of an unofficial debating theatre, particularly given the words on the sign - "for the use and pleasure of living birds". Many, including Cloud-Down herself, think that the echoing of 'pleasure' and 'life/living' between the sign and the Message is too much of a coincidence to *be* coincidence. And so the memorial has its own importance when it comes to understanding the Message.

Today, the weather is miserable. There are few pigeons at the memorial, much to Cloud-Down's disappointment. She could have stayed at home, kept dry, but instead she had come here in the hope that others might also brave the weather.

But the only other bird here is a seagull, more than twice the size of Cloud-Down. She eyes it.

Usually, any bird other than pigeons daring to land upon the memorial would be swiftly chased off. The memorial is not for them, just as the Message is not for them. That is something all pigeons still hold to, even the eccentrics.

And yet...

Cloud-Down hops a little closer to the seagull. It looks at her, tilting its head.

"What," it says flatly.

Cloud-Down blinks in surprise. She hadn't expected it to initiate the conversation.

"Hello," she says. "My name is Cloud-Down. Do

you know of a slab not far from here? With human writing on it?"

The seagull scoffs. "Of course I do. It's not like it's new."

That, Cloud-Down had not expected.

"Have you... have you heard of the Message?" she asks tentatively.

The seagull tilts its head. "The one none of you will share with us? That's written on the slab?"

"That one," Cloud-Down agrees. "Only - there's another line to the one we were taught. That isn't on the slab."

"Go on then," the seagull says.

Cloud-Down bobs her head. "The other line is this: *The bird has flown*."

"That's it?" the seagull asks after a moment. "That's your big secret? The one you like to lord over every other bird?"

Put like that, Cloud-Down supposes, it does sound a little bit ridiculous.

"We debate it," she offers. "Here, at the memorial. The whole Message. What it means."

"And I suppose that's why you chase us and the rest off."

"Yes," Cloud-Down admits. "But..." She hesitates, then decides; in for a sunflower seed, in for a sandwich. "I'm not sure we should, any more. If you've already seen most of the Message, then..."

"We discuss it, too," the seagull says. "Various ideas, lots of arguments. You know how it is."

"I do," Cloud-Down says, laughing. Then an idea strikes her.

226

"You could join us. Join the debate, see what ideas we can all form together."

"And be chased off again?" The seagull steps away. "I don't think so."

"We wouldn't," Cloud-Down promises. "I'd make sure of it. I think new ideas would be good for us, honestly. The next debate is probably tomorrow, if you did want to come."

"I'll think about it," the seagull says eventually. "Talk to the others. We'll see." She opens her wings to take off, then stops. "Call me Chip-Catch, by the way. If we're going to end up debating things." And then she's gone, shrieking away into the distance.

Cloud-Down watches her go.

She has a feeling that things are going to get very interesting.

22

Heather Turnbull

Emily

"I need you to come home Emily."

"I can't."

"Something's happened."

"Uh ha. Like I say I can't"

"I didn't want to do this over the phone...Dad died."

The bird has flown. My heart stopped momentarily, nausea hitting me like a wall, and I don't know why. Years of therapy and I revert instantly, needing his love, needing him. He can't be dead.

"I'm sorry for your loss, but it's not mine."

"Could you for once in your life not be a bitch about this."

"Fuck you."

"I don't know what went down between you two, but it was six years ago. I need my sister right now."

"You don't need me Josh."

As I press the red button to end the call I feel a release of emotions, I sit in the café sobbing as people watch on. I fight for breath, for control, but every time I get close it slips away. Furious with myself, and full of self-hatred I grab my coat and bag, fleeing my safe place for the solitude of outside.

On the train the light pierces through the dense woodland in flashing streams and I once again feel a void of emotion. Exhausted by the weight of everyone else's emotional responsibility. I sleep eventually, waking to change trains. England greets me and I feel a mixture of emotions in returning.

"Em!" Josh's arms embrace me, he softens me, weakens me.

"Hey."

"It's so good to have you home."

I nod. His wife, Rachel stands in the hallway watching me, her kind eyes telling me she knows how I feel, but I doubt that. As Josh steps back she steps in and embraces me and I feel like I could melt, spill it all. But I pull myself together.

As we sit eating her cake, I keep my eyes low. Suddenly feeling crushed by the weight of being here. Just as I get the courage to say I'm going to check into my hotel, Josh interrupts my thoughts. "We are going over to Dad's"

"Okay" I am shocked by my own words, I am not ready for that, not emotionally steady enough not to fall apart. The cake curdles in my stomach as I smile despite myself.

I can't believe it's been six years since I've been here. His home hasn't changed, dust filters through the light of the outside. Rachel walks past me pulling open the curtains and I shy my eyes and find myself unable to hide a smile as the action was something he'd do when I would open them. He preferred little light...no...he was paranoid, hiding behind these curtains from a world of things imagined by his genius.

229

My dad didn't believe in using computers, he wouldn't even own a phone, which, when your children are re-homed can become problematic for staying in touch. He'd write to us though.

Josh see's this man as one who was very mentally unwell. He was so young when we were re-housed that he settled well. He forgot our dad, not in the sense of contact but in his knowing of who he was. We were the lucky ones, our first foster home became our forever home, Phil and Marie nurtured us, put up with my rebellion and doted on Josh. I'd come back though, often, I'd sneak out and walk the ten plus miles to this place, desperate to see my dad.

"Most of this can probably go into the bin, the furniture might get taken on by a charity shop."

"What? No"

Rachel looks taken aback by my glare and Josh steps in, ever the peacekeeper. "Em, we have to have this place cleared out by a week Saturday"

"Why?"

"Because I sorted out an estate agent to come and value it." He sounds nervous, he should be, he's selling our dads house before he's even cold in his grave and I feel a piercing anger.

"I can't afford the funeral Em. We're not in a great situation, you look at me like I'm a monster, but you haven't even been home in six years!"

"It... it just felt fast."

Silence hangs between the three of us awkwardly.

"I can pay for the funeral, that's my job anyway," I swallow back my anger suddenly feeling the pressure I've inflicted on Josh, "I'm the oldest, none of this

230

should have fallen to you...sorry. Sorry Rach." She shakes her head and smiles as if to say no worries and Josh's shoulders release.

"Why don't we take stock of what's here today and I'll buy some boxes and bags so we can come and pack up during the week." They both nod. The awkwardness still hangs between us and so I move into Dad's office. Piles of papers, walls of books and a musty smell of old paper greets me. The second chair beside his desk is piled with old newspapers, it's my chair. He bought it for me so that we could work together on his latest case...or the ongoing one. I sit in his chair and look around the room, envious always of his book collection. I'd take them, I know Josh and Rachel wouldn't care, but I live out of a suitcase most of the time. I must have been sitting here for some time when Josh appeared at the door.

"Hey sis, can we go for a coffee?" He pauses and I know I won't like what he say's next "I'd also like to go to where he died and place some flowers."

"Why? He's not there you know."

"I know. It's kind of a tradition Rachels family have."

I want to fight it, but as I don't have a strong opinion on it, I let them do what they need to. We pick up flowers from Zonin along the coast road. I stand watching the sea and breathing in all the floral scents. I used to do this when I was a little girl. Whilst other children spent their money on sweets or magazines I'd go to the florist. It was so opposite to our home, fresh and colourful. They had a big image of crashing waves on the back wall and after a while the lady that owned the shop would let me sit and just be in it for a few moments. I bought cut flowers home to brighten it up, but I had to have them in my room. They made Dad too sad to have them in the central space, I think that was because of mum, but he never talked about her. Except occasionally when her would say I looked just like her. And then he'd close up once again.

Rachel buys a mixed bouquet, and we walk the streets to where dad died. I lag behind, unsure why I feel such unease as we approach this place, I don't believe my dad's spirit is here or that there is any significance to this. Perhaps it's the unexplained circumstance of his death that holds me. The coroner says it's a suspicious death. No witnesses have come forward. I hate that he died like this. I hate him for leaving. I feel so angry that I never came home. I can feel myself drowning in the overwhelming emotions, I don't even notice Josh and Rachel securing flowers to the lamppost. I walk looking at the floor steadying my breathing and then...*The bird has flown*...

I place my hand on the lamppost and Rachel steadies me, she sits me at the curb and is telling me to breathe, but she sounds so far away, and I feel confused. There's too many things going on in my head and I am not sure if I am going to cry or pass out. I hear my breathing and I am coming back, swimming to the surface. Josh and Rachel are crouching in front of me, concerned eyes flicked to me and then to one another.

"I'm okay." I say softly, and I don't feel like I'm lying. They go to stand me up, but I wave away their hands in slow motion, "I'll just sit here for a moment longer." They're whispering above me but don't care, I just need a moment. I find my breathing, find my calming image, and focus on it. I begin a body scan, slowly pulling myself back into the physical world. I stand again, it takes a lot and their hands steady me, making me feel like an invalid. I steady myself and nod. They carry on securing the flowers. I step back. And feel the hedge behind me. I look down. A moss-covered slab draws my attention, those words. THOSE WORDS! Before I realise it, I'm on the floor rubbing the dirt off of a paving slab and the words that have both excited and haunted me for all these years are here, engraved in a slab that looks hundreds of years old. I am filled with confusion. Why is this here? What does this mean? I'm muttering and Rachels hand on my shoulder is pulling me back but I'm spiralling. I must be having a break down, imagining things. I turn to Rachel with wild eyes. "Do you see that?"

"See what?" She is full of concern.

"The paving slab, the writing?"

She looks past me and reads it, nodding "Yes."

I breath and sit back on my heals, heart beating out of my chest, tears overspilling.

Josh is on the floor beside me, arms around me, holding me, rocking me. I hear Rachel on the phone behind me, she's distant and her voice echo's off in my head. I want Josh to look at the slab and tell me he knows what this is. "Read it josh." I manage behind tears.

"In search of true pleasure, how vainly we roam, to hold it for life, we must find it at home.

The Bird Has Flown."

"It's dad's big case."

He shakes his head blankly and I feel so alone.

I read the slab again and again. I take a picture on my phone and don't notice the growing crowd along the pavement or peering out of the window. An ambulance draws up and I find myself confused. The paramedics crouch beside me and talk to me, help me into the back of the ambulance and the warmth of the bed beneath me and the blanket around my shoulders comforts me. I come around enough to convince them that it is just the grief of the loss of my dad that has bought on this episode. My words come out like bubbles, I feel them float away and I know going in might be the best thing, but I can't, not now, not after seeing that. Josh and Rachel quietly protest the paramedics choice in letting me go. I ask them to drop me at my hotel and they protest again. I win. I assure them I will get rest and they leave me, eventually.

I sink into the bath unable still to understand what I have seen. What that where he'd got the message from? Was it all made up? He told me it was found in an archaeological exploration by one of our ancestors. He carried a cryptex he'd solved years ago with an ancient parchment in it that I was never allowed to see or touch; that parchment contained the same verses as that paving slab, almost. It was translated from ancient Egyptian, but the two messages were too close to imagine that they were separate. There was only one way to prove if he was telling the truth, I have to find the cryptex. I jump out of the bath feeling steady and suddenly very well. I check my handbag and check I still have Dad's keys.

Back in our home I search his office first, tip over piles of papers and rummage through drawers but its not here. "Where the fuck is it dad!" I shout into the emptiness and move to the next room. I've searched it all collapse on to the sofa full of frustration. When I couldn't find something as a child, I'd behave in much the same manner, screaming at dad to help of I'd be late for school. He'd come and sit on the sofa and tap the seat beside him. I'd rant a little longer before I joined him. I'd slam down on the sofa in a strop, arms folded, terrified of being late. "You have to sit, still yourself and it will come." He'd slide his hand down the side of the sofa and pull it out producing a shoe, or my keys and relief would sweep through me, "these sofas are secret hiding places for many treasures." I laugh into this empty space, feeling him beside me and I wonder...I slowly move my hand down the side of the sofa but there is nothing there. I stand and pull off all the cushions. A few bits of change, a sock, lint. "Don't forget to try right down the side of the seat" he'd say. My hand reaches down and a find something, a catch, a pull it and the side of the sofa comes out. The cryptex glints in the light, I lift in out and remember the code my father showed me. We'd never actually opened it together; he worried the air would deteriorate the paper. Anxiously when I hear the click, I pull back. I expect an empty tube but find a paper unlike anything I'd seen. The drawings beautiful. My father had taught me ancient hieroglyphs but there in this sheet was one I'd never seen a bird in flight.

I wept for the father I'd called mad when I left. Knowing that he wasn't. I hear him speak in the empty room, "We find it at home" and I know that I must keep this place. I have to finish his work.

23
Annie Hart

Common sense told her she should not be doing this. "I'm sorry, I'm sorry, I'm sorry. I promise I will sit down; we will sit down, lie down even and have a camomile tea and a rest. Honestly, just one more box, oh shit it's even heavier than the last one and I'll call it a day."

Bloody conveyancing why did it have to take so long. If things had kept to plan Jack would have been here too and the move down from Manchester to their new home on the south east coast would have been a piece of Sussex pond pudding, whatever that was she thought hungrily. Megan rummaged around the Waitrose carrier bags of groceries that she picked up enroute through Worthing to find something quick and easy to eat.

"You getting peckish as well baby?" She patted her ripening belly, just a few weeks away now from her expected delivery date. "What kind of mother am I? Clearly one that overtires and starves her offspring if it's anything to go by today's standards. Come on, a cracker and hummus for you, and a cracker and hummus for me and a camomile tea to soothe my threatened high blood pressure."

She took her tea into the garden of their new home and found a rusting wrought iron bench to sit on. The house was what the estate agent had referred to as, "traditionally Sussex". "These houses are some of the most desired on the market," he enthused. "Warm to the welcome, with their quality timber cladding and dependable red brick. Like a barn conversion, but more sophisticated." He sounded like he was reading off a script Megan and her husband Jack had chuckled at later.

But even so, maybe his smooth patter had had an effect on them. They'd been drawn to the house and especially to the unusual and quaint lychgate at the bottom of the front garden path. "Isn't that a usual feature of churches?" said Jack. "Be handy for food shop driver to leave the groceries if we're out."

"What was the original point of it?" asked Megan. "Actually, what can you tell us about the previous owners?"

But the young estate agent had no further information to offer and he changed the subject to point out the larger than average garden, that was laid out with mature shrubs and well stocked herbaceous borders that hummed with the seasonal business of a range of pollinators.

Megan noticed a swathe of the garden had been left for wildflowers to flourish freely like dandelions, plantain, yarrow and selfheal, she bent down to rub some leaves between her fingers and smelt the tang of lemon balm respected in the medicinal world for its efficaciousness as a remedy for heartache, anxiety and depression. She felt a tug of excitement at the thought of discovering what else those verdant beds contained for her to discover and make use of?

The move had been her husband Jack's idea, "I want our kids to have a different lifestyle to us," he said. "Just imagine, longer, lighter, dryer days, more space, countryside and seaside, paddle boarding, walks on the South Downs and fresh fish every day."

"Surf 'n' turf living. You make us sound like the family from Swallows and Amazons." Megan laughed.

"More like roosting pigeons and Amazon deliveries," said Jack.

And apart from this last section of their newly planned lifestyle it had seemed that fate was totally on their side. Jack's skills as a shrewd yet fair company lawyer were valued and his request to transfer to the group's commutable London office was well received. But part of his workload was dealing with the company merger and that had revealed unforeseen incompatible commercial cultures which threatened to overshadow its main business aims. The need to untangle multiple processes and procedures had meant that Jack had to stay in the north west until the joining of the companies had fully completed.

"You owe me big time matey boy," said Megan. "That babymoon had better be good."

And so, it had fallen to Megan to project manage the entire move from their home in Chorlton cum Hardy in the suburbs of Manchester made even trendier – if blunting its tradition swagger and edginess in the process - by the swathes of journalists and production company personal at BBC Salford that had moved up over the last few years. The butcher had turned into an organic deli, and the ironmonger, launderette and off licence became bars where happy hour was as limitless as the jugs of prosecco. Megan and Jack's favourite pre pregnancy was no nonsense named, The Manc, which had: *Be different, just like everyone else* picked out in copperplate gold signwriting above the architrave like a power slogan from Victorian times.

But at least she had the luxury of time if not energy. Megan had already decided to take a career break. Since qualifying over twelve years ago as a speech therapist her interest in phytomedicine had begun to grow apace with every passing season. Once the baby, who remained nameless to date, but was jokingly referred to as The Squab was 18 months old or so she would start her studies at the College of Naturopathic Medicine in nearby Brighton. At least, that's what she had decided.

"This herbal hubble bubble toil and trouble stuff you want to study, babe. Seriously, are you sure?" said Jack. "It was your head for science and logic that attracted me. Well, that and your gorgeous eyes and cute arse," said Jack, pulling her into a hug.

"It is scientific, well, much of it. Where do you think some prescription medicines comes from? Then there's caffeine, morphine, cocaine," said Megan wriggling out of his grasp to pour a glass of kombucha from a Mason jar on the counter top. Yet another aspect of her new lifestyle she'd had to persuade a reluctant jack to take on who thought the fermenting scoby looked like a pickled alien.

"Now you're talking," said Jack.

"Oh yeah, you big geeky square, you've never so much as had a pull on a roll up and now you're trying to sound like Russell Brand in his hedonistic heyday. And don't knock the power of placebo," said Megan.

"Alright, but no dream catchers in the bedroom, right? And I don't want you going all sound baths and chanting on me and taking that Brighton vibe too far, tolerant and inclusive tick, experimental and whiffing of patchouli oil, no chuffing' way."

Her first night alone in the house had passed peacefully. She woke feeling rested and listened for a while to the cooing of wood pigeons in the yew trees and the lack of traffic sounds. "We're like their urban cousins Squab," she said to belly, "We were the feral ones and now we've hightailed it to the country."

Megan got up and from the still to be unpacked boxes and rails of clothes found something clean and fairly co-ordinated to wear for her antenatal check-up at the local GPs surgery. The mellow sunlight gave her new surroundings a more subtle clarity that her two previously visits in the glare and broil of summer had lacked. What she loved about autumn was its seasonal decay, it's last gasp of productivity, as the year built up to its final offerings of harvest bounty from the fields, allotments, orchards and hedgerows.

The practice midwife called her in with a cheery wave. "So, it'll be a hospital delivery? Or are you braving it at home depending on where you are. I take

241

it you're not living in a yurt near Cissbury Ring? We get all sorts of requests y'know after all this is Sussex," she said with a twinkle. "Oh sorry, forgetting myself there, it's Rose, you know, my name is... and all that."

The midwife flicked through several screens on her PC. "Let's check your address, ahhh, I know where you are. You've moved into the house just out of the village on the edge of the copse haven't you? The one with the lychgate and the carving." she said.

"That's three yeses to the address, lychgate and home birth and a no to the stone. We only, well, I only moved in last week and I've only just found the kettle let alone some mystery feature the estate agent failed to point out."

"Just you? There's no...?"

"Yes, there's a husband too but he's delayed on business. Only Manchester, should make it for the birth. Joke! He'll definitely be around for that. Sorry you were saying something about the lychgate?" said Megan.

"Oh, don't mind me. It's just that... Look, I'm back-to-back this morning so let's get you up on the examination table and see how everything progressing. Nothing to concern yourself about," said Rose.

"No worries, I've had more of these check-ups than I care to think about. Who knew I'd get so much unasked for attention as a so called geriatric pregnant woman?" said Megan.

"That wasn't that I meant," said Rose, "Now, relax this may feel a bit uncomfortable." She grimaced at the speculum as if it held a few rather more personal memories for herself.

Megan returned home with Rose's half told mention of the lychgate and whatever else she was talking about doing circuits in her head. The remaining time of her antenatal appointment was taken up with blood samples and asking for another prescription for folic acid and vitamin D. Megan was reluctant to take up anymore of the midwife's precious time than necessary on related matters especially as Rose had sealed off that line of conversation.

Where was the carving? And what if anything was significant about it? Had Jack seen it and just not mentioned it? They'd had such little time to talk in the last few weeks, he was working practically round the clock, and she was exhausted after the final hand over of all her speech therapy cases and what seemed like endless household packing.

As Megan walked down the lane to her home, she wondered why they hadn't looked into the feature of the lychgate – why was it there? Who decided to build it? What was its purpose? She and Jack just thought it was a quirky extra detail to the garden, like putting up a rather more detailed pergola or a bit of twist on a summerhouse. Now she felt a strange chill about it. "Stop being so dramatic, you're overtired and you probably need to up your iron intake and go easy on the unpacking there's no rush."

She opened the lychgate and eased herself down onto the bench that ran the length of the porch-like structure, the clay tiled roof was supported by four upright beams. She could now see that there was a

243

pattern at the top on all four sides, no, she realised not a pattern, they were parts of words but years of weathering and the growth of ivy made it impossible to read the whole quotation. All she could make out was: *In search... plea... hold... for life...This bird... flown.*

What could it mean? "This is a step ladder jobby and a scrub at the foliage," she thought determinedly. But that would be one of her most stupid ideas of all. The brickwork on the floor of the lychgate was already slippy made worse by the easy to trop on threadbare covering of moss and roots. What a combination: nearly nine months pregnant, balancing on a wobbly stepladder on a slippery floor, in the fading light. What could possibly go wrong?

Anyways, she asked herself, what was a lychgate doing in a residential setting? She could at least settle that in her mind. Megan tapped into her mobile phone: Wiki does a lychgate have a purpose? Within seconds she had her answer: *Typically, they are gabled or hipped roofed, often with benches where mourners could sit, or with a lych-stone, coffin stool or trestle, upon which a coffin could be rested.*

Stupid or not a pale faced, heart swiftly beating Megan walked with her hand on her belly towards the house to fetch the stepladder as the baby fluttered inside her like it was testing its wings.

Introducing the Real Press...

Take a look at our other publications at ...

www.therealpress.co.uk

http://bit.ly/HowToBecomeAFreeance
Writer

Printed in Great Britain
by Amazon

84924499R00144